Femme
CONFIDENTIAL

Femme
CONFIDENTIAL

Nairne Holtz

INSOMNIAC PRESS

Library and Archives Canada Cataloguing in Publication

Holtz, Nairne, 1967-, author
Femme confidential / Nairne Holtz.

Issued in print and electronic formats.
ISBN 978-1-55483-193-7 (softcover).--ISBN 978-1-55483-197-5 (PDF)

I. Title.

PS8615.O484F46 2017   C813'.6   C2017-904147-9
                                              C2017-904148-7

The publisher gratefully acknowledges the support of the Canada
Council for the Arts and the Ontario Arts Council.

Printed and bound in Canada

Insomniac Press
520 Princess Avenue, London, Ontario, Canada, N6B 2B8
www.insomniacpress.com

The following stories, which have been woven into this novel, have
previously been published in a quite different form: "Miss August," in
Back to Basics: a butch-femme anthology (Bella, 2004) and "Most
Valuable Player," in *Best Lesbian Erotica 2011* (Cleis, 2010).

The Canada Council | Le Conseil des Arts
FOR THE ARTS | DU CANADA
SINCE 1957 | DEPUIS 1957

ONTARIO ARTS COUNCIL
CONSEIL DES ARTS DE L'ONTARIO

To butches and femmes everywhere

A number of people made this book so much better.
My editor at Insomniac Press, Gillian Rodgerson, was
perceptive and dogged; Lucy Jane Bledsoe, Zsuzsi
Gartner, and Megan Holtz provided useful commentary;
librarians Sanja Petrovic and Tammy Danciu helped with
details, as did Luca Rueter, Rebecca Emerson, and Tracy
Ford; Jessica Harris did all of the above; and, for the years
of conversations about sex and love, I'd like to thank my
femme confidante, Miriam Ginestier.

Parkdale I

Toronto, 2014

I got off the streetcar a couple of stops past my house to go to the bank. As the machine dispensed my bills, an odour of pee filtered up. Homeless people sometimes slept on the floor beside the cash machines. I'd lived in the Toronto neighbourhood of Parkdale for almost twenty-five years and watched its trajectory from sketchy to hip, or perhaps sketchy *and* hip would be a better way to put it. Amidst the funky foodie joints and health food stores and bars serving craft beer were community-service agencies, high-rises the police regularly visited, and this particular corner. While a bar whose clientele had been winos, working girls, and pimps had long since been replaced by a succession of takeout food establishments, at least one of which went bankrupt every year, there was also a thrift store on the south side of Queen that had been around forever along with the Coffee House, where Toronto's older recovery crowd hung out. Not in the café but outside it, smoking and sometimes going off on each other.

As I headed east towards the little house my wife and I owned, I spotted Sophia, who was going to look after our dogs on the weekend. Sophia was absorbed in her device and didn't hear me call her name. It wasn't until I touched her shoulder that I got her attention.

"Liberty! I didn't see you," she said.

"Indeed," I replied. "Riveting texts?"

She blushed, something I hadn't seen her do before. Sophia was an opinionated, bookish teenager. It was both a surprise and a relief to her mothers, an ex-club kid and ex-raver, that Sophia was more interested in reading political blogs on Tumblr than partying. Perhaps the fact that her father was in rehab again took the romance out of drugs.

"I was looking at Tinder," Sophia explained.

"I've heard about that," I said. "It's Grindr for straight people, right?"

"It's not just straight and it's not just hooking up."

"Can I see it?"

Sophia stopped and showed me the Tinder app on her phone. With quick finger swipes, she rejected three face shots of young men and displayed a photo gallery of boys and girls whom she hadn't rejected. All the cool urban high school kids were genderqueer these days—we can date anyone and we don't care about gender! Sophia's lesbian moms thought their social-justice-minded daughter probably wasn't queer, but who knew for sure? Sophia's adolescence was so different from theirs, from mine. When I was a teenager, the idea of being a dyke had scared the hell out of me. I remembered thinking I might be one and consciously burying it—deciding to wait until I left home to sleep with a girl. I was already such a freak; being gay was too much to take on.

"How do you have time to meet all these people?" I asked as Sophia scrolled through screen after screen of cute young things.

She looked at me like I was an idiot. The one generational constant is kids telling parents how out of touch they (the parents) are, with plenty of metaphorical and literal eye rolling. She informed me she had only been on one date with a guy from Tinder. "It was really awkward, and I told him I didn't want to go on another one."

"I see," I said. And I did. I remembered awkward—getting drunk to have sex and not being able to talk about it. I especially remembered how awkward I'd felt when I met her stepmother, Veronika.

Break-In

Toronto, 1990

Veronika had dyed black hair that was a fucked-up combination of shaved and long, but her ragged hair and gravelly voice and collection of oversized concert T-shirts stolen from the different boys she had screwed couldn't hide how small and pretty she was, small and pretty and mean. Her meanness was a problem because I wanted to be tender. I wanted to gaze into her eyes that were like dark, wet rocks in a stream, and run the tip of my finger over her glossy lips. Imagining this embarrassed me. It was cheesy and she would laugh at me, and she did enough of that already. Also, I didn't think she was gay. Then again, I didn't think I was either. Or, well, I guess I didn't know.

It was summer and I was twenty and so was she, and we had met at the twenty-four-hour diner where I worked. I'd brush by her with bus pans of dishes while she entertained various guys, dealers and deejays and bouncers who kept her supplied with booze and drugs and got her into clubs. It was embarrassing seeing her there because I looked like crap. My curly blonde-brown Peter Frampton hair was stuffed under a hairnet, and I was invariably sweaty and red-faced with fogged-up glasses and a greasy apron. A man's polyester uniform hid my body, but for some reason she was nicer to me at work than when I ran into her at a club, showered and dressed up.

Maybe she was sweeter at the diner because she wasn't as drunk. I couldn't figure it out. One time she followed me into the alley, where I was throwing a bag of garbage into the dumpster, and told me about how she and this guy had broken into a summer cottage and fucked on the floor. Since I didn't really know her, I thought it was strange she was telling me this, but what was weirder was the look in those dark eyes of hers, like she was daring me. But what was she daring me to do? Judge her?

I was in no place to judge anyone. A few months earlier I'd hitchhiked to Toronto from Nova Scotia with this guy named Donny, and neither of us had money or a place to stay. He started tricking while I scrounged for change in fountains because I was too embarrassed to beg, and didn't want to do what he was doing. I had $45, no bank account, no credit card, no parents willing to bail me out.

My parents were punishing me for leaving university. They had loved their undergrad experience at a New England liberal arts college in the late sixties. They reminisced about staying up all night talking about Vietnam and civil rights and philosophy and aesthetics, and how they had discovered the Bloomsbury Group, with whom they were obsessed. Well, in 1988, students at a small-town university in Nova Scotia didn't talk about shit like that. They worried about whether they would get jobs, whether they would have to leave the province. My classmates were fine, as were my classes and grades, but I didn't feel as though I belonged. I could have put up with that, seeing as I'd never felt as if I belonged anywhere, but just before Christmas in my second year, I was laid off from a part-time job it had taken me months to find. To stay at school, I would need to take out yet another loan.

I finished my exams, went home for the holidays, and on New Year's Eve met a guy named Donny at Halifax's alternative dance bar. He was taking dance classes and eked out a living stripping for men two nights a month at a tavern called the Lighthouse. He was looking for a roommate, and I moved into his second-floor walk-up and found a filing job at a used-car lot. In April I showed up at work to find chains and locks on all the doors—the place was bankrupt.

My parents considered my job loss as further evidence of my poor judgment—they had never lost a job. I was their daughter but not a cause they believed in, and they refused to lend me money to cover my rent. Donny couldn't cover it on his own and his mom was on welfare, so we decided to do a runner and hitchhike to Toronto—more work, bigger scene. Donny was mostly gay, and I wondered about myself. We had kissed at the bar on New Year's Eve, but back at his place when he asked if I wanted to have sex, I said no and he said "me either." So we didn't have sex; we smoked a J and ate some popcorn, and the sun smeared through the window and everything in my life was a mess but felt all right.

Toronto without money was tough. I ate one meal a day at the Krishna temple, walked everywhere, scrambled to find a job, and crashed in an anarchist house, at some gay guy's condo, and on the couch of a girl I met. One night I slept in the waiting room of a hospital.

Being that broke was scary, but Veronika scared me almost as much. "He ripped my panties off," she had told me, looking me right in the eye. What girl says "panties" in a sexy way to another girl? Was she coming on to me? Did I want her to?

The club where Veronika hung out was the Labyrinth, a place on Queen West that catered to all sexual types, but mostly exhibitionists. She'd stand at the edge of the dance floor in her too big T-shirts and her too short cut-offs, checking out the handful of dykes. If a woman came over with a second drink in hand, she'd instantly huddle up to her gay male friends. She let me get closer, maybe because we liked the same loud, raunchy music. When Jane's Addiction or Sisters of Mercy came on, we'd collide into each other on the dance floor as though we were in a mosh pit. We'd yell out the chorus of our favourite Pixies song to each other, "Is she weird, is she white, is she promised to the night." But it could get boring, dancing and waiting for Queen Veronika to pay attention to me. One night, I decided to leave early.

Veronika waved at me with her cigarette, and I came over.

"You're going?" she asked.

"Uh-huh."

"To another club?"

"Home." It felt good to say that word.

She reached over and pointlessly or not so pointlessly tucked the bottom of my T-shirt into my black cotton skirt, her knuckles gliding over my stomach.

I looked at her. "Do you like girls?"

She took her hand out of my waistband. "You mean, am I into you?"

There was no point in denying it. "Yes."

"What do you think?" was her non-answer.

I left. She didn't really like me, I decided. She just got off on having power over me.

A few days later, I came home from work, and my roommate told me someone had broken into our place.

"It's weird because nothing got stolen," she said. "Maybe the person was too fucked up and forgot what they came for."

Parkdale, where we lived, was full of what my roommate called "people with issues." Victorian and Edwardian mansions in the once grand neighbourhood had been turned into rooming houses or razed and replaced by apartment buildings—cheap housing that attracted immigrants, refugees, ex-cons, and mental patients turfed out of a nearby institution the government had stopped funding. Amidst so many people wanting to escape their grim reality, a drug scene bloomed. Our apartment above a laundromat on Queen Street was in the centre of the action. Last time I'd washed my clothes, a guy sitting on the floor lit up a crack pipe.

I went into my bedroom and saw my journal lying open on my futon. *I can't deal with this*, I thought, and took a shower. When I crawled into bed, I recognized the lingering scent of Coco Chanel perfume and Camel cigarettes and realized who the trespasser was. Veronika knew where I lived because she knew my roommate, had gone to parties at my place before I'd moved in. Her handwriting in my journal was about three times the size of mine: "Don't worry, I didn't read your diary. Well, just a few pages. I don't want to be a taker, but I don't have anything to give." A quashing postscript followed: "You're such a hippie!"

I hadn't told Veronika my parents were hippies, but if having a noun for a first name—Liberty—hadn't suggested this, perhaps my meagre furnishings had. They were a little granola for a girl who had been crashing at a squat: an Indian cotton bedspread on the wall, red candles, and an incense holder on the windowsill. Sometimes I liked to be lulled by what was soft and bright and smelled good.

I didn't know whether to feel violated or flattered by her behaviour; I felt both. I thought about that story she'd told me about breaking into a house, and I imagined her naked on the floor, being fucked by some guy. I put my hands between my legs and came in a long, tight string of orgasms.

The next day, I stole a tin from work and bought some fortune cookies. I removed the fortunes, crossed out sayings about auspicious events, and wrote in tiny letters "cunnilingus doesn't suck." Then I stuffed the revised fortunes into the crack of each cookie. When I saw her at the diner, I handed her the tin and didn't leave the kitchen until she was gone.

She stopped coming to the diner. She was pretending not to want anything from me. I was a girl, but she made me feel like a guy, a pathetic one, and I hated it. I avoided her, too: I quit going to Labyrinth, and locked my bedroom window. I would keep her out; I would keep away from her. Too bad, she kept barging into my brain. Before and after my shifts, I'd head to my favourite café where I'd drink cappuccinos and twirl my hair around my finger and write about her in my journal. I thought about ripping out the page she had written on but didn't. At night I fantasized about her. Not regular sex, not kissing her or going down, but rougher scenes like the two of us getting busted for possession and being sent to jail. She, naked, her warm skin pressed against the cold metal bars of the cell, and me fucking her from behind, my fingers inside her while a dykey-looking screw watched us.

One afternoon at the café, a slender creature with sleek red hair and a white jumpsuit strode up to my table, handed me a gold lipstick, and strode off before I could say a word. The lipstick was Currant Stain by Yves St. Laurent, and when I rolled up the tube, I discovered a tiny piece of paper. There was a message for me, two words: "Prove it."

Apparently, neither of us was as not gay as I had thought.

The next day, Veronika showed up at the diner as I was getting off my shift. We wandered around Queen Street, went into a few stores, had a few drinks at a bar. An old guy came over to us and placed his hands on our table: "You girls are talking, talking, talking. You're either sisters or dykes. Which is it?"

It wasn't a question. I stood up. "None of your fucking business."

We went back to my place. Veronika made herself comfortable on my futon, her hand twisting through my roommate's cat's fur. I took the cat and tossed it out the door.

"Why'd you do that?" she asked.

I sat down on the edge of the futon. "I got your message from the red-haired girl."

"She's a he. You're the only girl I hang out with," she said, gazing intently at her long fingernails with their black nail polish and silver biker rings.

I picked up her hand, and she tugged it away and stood

up to examine a pile of books the previous occupant had left behind. *Catcher in the Rye* was on the top, and she chucked it across the room. She was kind of melodramatic.

I raised an eyebrow and she glared at me.

"I hate *Catcher in the Rye*! I can't believe you have it. God, everyone at my stupid alternative high school was into that book. The main character, what's his name, is this depressed homophobe."

How could she refer to homophobia and be so skittish with me? "Was there anything gay in that book?"

Veronika flung herself onto my futon. "You don't remember the guy freaking out about his teacher making a pass at him?"

I shook my head. I had read the book when I was sixteen, and at that time I hadn't paid so much attention to gay stuff. I knew I was sexually attracted to women but never imagined this desire could eclipse men. Books about English boarding schools were full of girls getting crushes on each other, and it didn't seem to mean much. Now, with a girl I wanted lying beside me on my bed, I realized it could mean everything.

I told Veronika I had read all of Salinger in two weeks, that I liked *Franny and Zooey* best, and she looked unimpressed. A girl into degradation probably wouldn't find much appeal in a heroine who was obsessed with spiritual purification. I was so nervous I yammered on about the book anyway. I also told her I had studied English literature for a while at a university in Nova Scotia. "How about you?"

"Dropout."

I frowned. "You dropped out of high school?"

Pow. She punched my arm.

"No, dummy, same as you, university. I started a commerce degree."

I wasn't expecting that and I laughed, and she made a sour face. I rubbed my arm while she took her Camel cigarettes out of her handbag, which was made from black rubber and covered in black rubber spikes, S&M chic. She tapped her ashes onto my incense holder without asking permission.

"I should have studied theatre. That's what my family thought I'd go into."

Her parents had expected her to be an actress? Were they as unconventional as mine? "What does your dad do?"

"Why do you care?"

I shrugged. I was trying to place her. To figure out if she was fucked up or if it was more of a pose.

"My father doesn't *do* anything. He's dead." She gave me a creepy clown smile and took another drag of her cigarette.

Was she telling the truth? I lay on my back on my bed, not speaking, while Veronika lined herself up next to me. It occurred to me that we were both lonely.

I moved my leg so our thighs were touching, and she let me, watching to see what I'd do next. I held out my hand, and she gave me her cigarette and I butted it out. She put her arms above her head, an animal showing me her belly, her meanness on hold.

I took off my glasses and got on top of her, and we began to neck. I ran my hand along the inside of her leg, slipping my fingers through a hole in her jean shorts. "I think you're really sexy."

"How seductive."

I didn't like how sarcastic her tone was. I kissed her again so she'd shut up, but also because I wanted reassurance. We kissed and rubbed against each other. It grew a little monotonous, and I was wondering if we should stop when she sat up and removed her clothes. I took off mine as well. Timidity hung in the air thick as incense. We didn't know what to do. We shyly peeked at each other, and then she pushed me onto my back. The warm weight of her as she licked my nipples was lovely. I ran my hands along the slope of her buttocks and was struck by the softness. Then Veronika did something hard. Crawled between my legs and took a mouthful of my pubic hair and tugged on it with her teeth.

The jolt of pain slicing through my arousal was almost interesting, but I didn't want her to hurt me because it was too close to how she acted towards me generally.

"Ow," I told her a beat too late. "Stop."

"You hurt me, then," she said.

She'd hurt me so I'd hurt her. "I don't want to hurt you." This wasn't entirely true: She was a brat, and part of me wanted to smack her ass and fuck her hard. Another part of me was scared and didn't want to. What I really wanted from her was so huge I could never ask for it—I wanted her to love me.

She stood up, and I noticed her breasts hung down. Mine were more flat champagne glasses. I always ranked other girls' attractiveness against mine, figuring out where we stood in the hierarchy of pretty, but if I fucked women, if I were a lesbian, I wouldn't have to do this, and that felt like such a relief. I could just love women, not compete with them. We could both be beautiful, except Veronika seemed oblivious towards my slender body. It held no power over her—I could tell—and I both wanted to have power over her and wanted us to stop playing these power games.

"Do you have any booze?" Veronika asked.

I went to the fridge and stole some beer from my roommate, making a mental note to buy her some the next day.

I found Veronika sitting on my futon with her legs spread. Instead of handing her the beer, I impulsively held the cold, damp can between her legs. She gasped (in a good way), and I put the can down and stuck my fingers in her.

"Fuck me," she said. For the first time all evening, we were in sync. We were no longer jester and queen.

She reached down and touched her clit with her middle fingers. Using just her finger pads, she angled her nails so they were pointed upwards, away from her tender flesh. *So that's how girls with long nails masturbate*, I thought.

"I'm coming," she moaned. "Harder." I pushed my hand in and out of her, and as her cunt gripped me, her face became animal.

Afterwards, she said, "That felt good." She laughed like she was surprised.

"I guess that's the advantage of sleeping with another woman," I said. "We know how to please each other."

"I didn't come with the other girl I slept with."

I wasn't her first? Why had she made it so hard for me? I opened my mouth to ask and stopped when I realized I didn't want to know. I also didn't want to admit I'd never done it with a woman before.

We got into T-shirts and crawled into bed. She rolled onto her stomach, ready for sleep, and I wondered why she wasn't touching me. Was I just supposed to be grateful? I slipped my hand between my legs and snuck a look at her. She was watching me through half-closed lids, and gave my thigh an encouraging squeeze. Feeling self-conscious, I closed my eyes and made myself come, a ring of pleasure twisting free. Cool air rushed over me—Veronika had flung off the sheet. I opened my eyes and watched as she oh so solemnly bent down and kissed the top of my pussy. It was the closest either of us would ever get to going down on each other.

Her restless body woke me a few hours later. She told me she was going to the can when really she was leaving my apartment. Leaving me.

Under a Spell

Ontario, 1986

During middle school, Veronika watched how other kids talked and acted, then imitated them. Inside, she felt small and nervous, as though she were on the verge of exposure while not being sure what it was she didn't want other kids to see. She was like an undercover spy who had forgotten her mission. But she got fed up with trying to fit in, and during high school decided she was the cool one and that the kids at her school were the losers. None of them had heard of her favourite bands, Adam and the Ants, Generation X.

At sixteen she started taking five-hour return bus trips to Toronto, where she had lived until she was eleven. She'd head up to Bathurst and Bloor to buy sour cherry strudel at the Hungarian cafés. Her mother wasn't much for cooking, and Veronika's childhood memories involved more takeout Chinese than goulash, but she liked seeing other Hungarians, hearing them speak the language. When her father was alive, her parents spoke it whenever they didn't want her to understand, but she'd learned some anyway.

From Bloor Street, she'd walk to Kensington Market to try on suede jackets and old-fashioned dresses and see the punks. One afternoon, she had followed a girl for a few blocks. The girl had black hair worn in a bob and was dressed all in black: her sweater, skirt, tights, and shoes.

She even wore black lipstick; her mouth was like a dark tulip. *What would it be like to show up at school like that, to choose to be weird rather than have people decide I am?*

Veronika dyed her dark-brown hair blue-black and purchased goth clothes at a store called Lovely Tragedy. Her classmates' response to her new look was swift and hostile. Boys mocked her—think it's Halloween, bitch?—and girls were unfriendly or uncomfortable. The R.G.T.A. girls didn't seem to notice. They were the girls who wore Lacoste shirts, dated the cutest jocks and preppies, played sports or were in the year-end musical (*Guys and Dolls*, *Jesus Christ Superstar*, *Anne of Green Gables*), and had the phrase "Remember Good Times Always" beside their yearbook pictures.

Veronika wasn't sure which she hated more: the system of popularity or being irrelevant. Following election speeches for class president, students were invited to ask the candidates questions, and Veronika went to the microphone and challenged the rich preppy guy everyone knew was going to win. She said, "You claim to represent the interests of all students. How can you when you're a preppy who just hangs out with preppies?" A thunder crack of applause broke out, surprising Veronika, who had no idea so many other kids felt the way she did. Her attack didn't change the outcome of the election (the other candidate being a nerd), but she obtained a new status and her own acronym: G.W.H.P.— Girl Who Hates Preppies. A few people were admiring; others were nasty. R.G.T.A. ignored her, but at least they knew who she was.

She was still alone. Sweet sixteen (though in her opinion there was nothing fucking sweet about it) and never been kissed, even though Oscar, the spirit of her Ouija board, had predicted she would get a boyfriend in high school. The planchette glided firmly and directly to yes under her fingers whenever she posed the question. She supposed she could get a boyfriend if she lowered her standards. Her mother said she was the prettiest girl in their extended family, and guys often checked her out. Not boys at school so much, because they thought she was too strange, but older guys— the father of one of the kids she babysat, college-age boys during her bus rides to Toronto, her French teacher, and Hungarians at the bizarre ball her mother had once made her attend at the Hungarian House. No one she could imagine kissing.

Would a love spell help her? They weren't easy to find. At the Toronto Occult Shop there were lots of books about witches but no practical information about casting spells. Feminist authors described female covens that performed rituals to celebrate nature, while the author of *The Satanic Bible* counselled aspiring witches to wear spiked heels (Veronika did have a pair of boots with spiked heels) and garter belts (that just seemed too *Penthouse*). She was ready to give up when she found what she was looking for in a grocery store. On a metal rack by the cash register, beside some horoscope books, was a pocket book entitled *Love Spells*. Real spells with instructions and lists of ingredients! Ingredients she could find, as opposed to unhelpful references to mandrake root.

On a night when she had the house to herself, she undressed in the upstairs bathroom, which was as large as her bedroom had been in Toronto, and began her spell. Lit a white candle and set it on the toilet lid. Filled the claw-foot tub with water and scattered rose petals on the surface.

Climbed into the tub and stared into the candle flame and visualized her future lover. A boy who looked like Billy Idol, whose mouth she couldn't stop watching in his videos, the way his lips went from bee-stung pout to animal-that-could-swallow-her sneer. A rock star in black leather, a bad boy was what she wanted. Not to reform, but a fellow wolf to run with, to dispel the boredom that she experienced as a constant low-grade sickness.

A week later at the mall, Veronika was shoplifting when she heard a voice say, "You stealing something?"

The mascara she was about to tuck into her purse clattered to the floor. "I'm not doing anything," she whined.

"Yeah, right."

Oh God, it was Perry, who went to her school. Chubby Chippewa guy with a moon face and long black hair pulled into a ponytail. Every day it seemed he wore the same T-shirt with Rick James' face on the front. Like her, he smoked, so they were part of the same crowd hanging out at the front steps, grabbing butts on breaks.

Perry's eyes flicked over to a uniformed security guard. "Let's get out of here."

Veronika didn't want to get busted, so she pretended to be Perry's friend, to be interested in what he was yakking on about, which was some sort of theory about school being bad for you because it teaches you to be obedient. When they reached the fountain in the middle of the mall, he asked her if she wanted to go for a smoke.

Veronika looked at her watch. Her bus didn't come for

another forty minutes. "Why not?"

He led her down the corridor and into a store she had never been in or even noticed, Walpert Tobacconists. The narrow, dimly lit shop was lined with dark-wood shelves that held boxes of cigars, packages of cigarettes, pipes, and large glass jars of loose tobacco that had an agreeable woodsy scent. Behind a long counter, a girl stood on a stepladder with her back to them, restocking the inventory. Perry called up to her: "Can you get me a pack of Player's?"

The girl retrieved the cigarettes and placed them on the counter, cupping them protectively. "You still owe me for the last pack."

Perry leaned forward and the two kissed. With tongue no less, gross. Veronika recognized his girlfriend as someone she knew from Girl Guides, Sharon Witkowski. Veronika had always been curious about her. She was scrawny with small pointy features and white-blonde hair flowing down her back. An aloof but not unkind tomboy, Sharon was quick to master knots and first-aid techniques that she silently demonstrated to the most hopeless girls. She always waited for a bus to take her home instead of getting picked up. She would smoke at the bus stop, as though she were an adult with a perfect right to do this, and, before long, quit Guides and was said to have quit school.

"We're going to the food court for a smoke," Perry told Sharon, gesturing to Veronika. "Want me to get you a coffee?"

Sharon shook her head. "Nah, I'm good."

Veronika piped up, "I used to be in Guides with you."

"I remember," Sharon replied shortly.

She and Perry exchanged another long kiss. Veronika

had never been French kissed, but it sounded like a disgusting hybrid of spitting and kissing. Frankly, she thought Sharon could do better than Perry. Her unwillingness to be friendly was also disappointing.

Veronika was grounded, which, since it was summer, really sucked. The conditions of her sentence were: babysitting was permitted, the mall and public pool were forbidden for two weeks, and she couldn't go to Toronto for six months, which was insane. How could she have a boyfriend if she couldn't see him? Except that was the reason she was in so much trouble.

She had wanted to go to an all-ages show in Toronto, but of course there was no way her mother would let her do something in Toronto at night, so Veronika arranged to sleep over at her cousin's place. Her cousin was younger, and they weren't particularly close, but Veronika talked her into going to the show. As they approached the club, her cousin freaked out. She looked around at the kids waiting in line, older teenagers in ripped jeans and black leather jackets. Some had shaved their heads, others had hair dyed crayon colours. "There's no way I'm going in there," her cousin announced. "Not with those people."

Veronika couldn't believe it. "It'll be fun. Don't be such a baby."

"I'm going home."

"No, you're not," Veronika said distractedly. Standing in front of her was Billy Idol. Not the real Billy but a boy her age with spiked blond hair, lips smeared with maraschino cherry lipstick, and wrists wound with studded strips of black leather. Her spell had worked! She tapped him on the shoulder and bummed a light and didn't notice her cousin steal off and creep onto the streetcar. When she realized what had happened, Veronika moaned about it to Billy Idol, whose actual name was Stefan.

"Maybe you should go," he suggested.

"I'll never catch up to her. I may as well stay and have fun."

The show was rad, though Veronika was more into it than Stefan, who said he was a poseur, into punk for the fashion. Inexplicably, he liked Pink Floyd. Had Veronika seen the movie, *The Wall*? She had seen it. What she mostly remembered was animation of female genitalia swallowing up a man crouched in the corner.

"It seemed like the main guy in it was afraid of women," Veronika told Stefan.

"Yes, because relationships are another prison," he replied. "The whole movie is about how life is a prison. You march into a bin, get ground up like sausage. You're just"—he lifted his fingers into quotes—"another brick in the wall."

After the show, after they tried unsuccessfully to get into a booze can, he took her north on the subway to his house, where he stole rum from his parents' liquor cabinet while she waited in the backyard. They went down the street to a graveyard, where they took turns gulping the rum. It warmed and loosened Veronika, who lay splayed out on top of a vault, pretending to be dead. She exposed her neck to Stefan.

"Bite me," she said.

He did, and she pulled him down and kissed him. He looked surprised but kissed her back. French kissing wasn't so gross after all. She liked the feeling of being under him, though it made her nervous. What if he wanted to do something she wasn't ready for? The idea of handling his penis freaked her out, even though she remembered an older cousin comparing it to a hot cabbage roll.

He mostly stuck to kissing. Gripped her ass but didn't touch her boobs or further down. Didn't even have a hard-on, which she had once felt during a slow dance. Her anxiety shifted to boredom. Did he think touching her vagina was as strange as she thought touching his dick was? She couldn't help remembering a phrase from a *Penthouse Forum* magazine she had read at a place where she babysat: wet blonde fur. Was that what Sharon's pubic hair would look like? Veronika tried to put the thought out of her mind, but the obscene phrase blinked and buzzed in her brain like a neon sign: wet blonde fur, wet blonde fur.

Veronika asked Stefan if he was a virgin.

"What do you think?" He sounded pissed off and something else—whiny. A touch aggressively, he asked, "Aren't you?"

"Yeah." Not because she was pure and good but because no one cool had hit on her.

"I have to take a leak." Stefan got up and jogged away behind a tree.

Veronika brushed a tiny twig from her dress and waited for him. He took her to the bus station, and she dragged him into a dark corner to neck, but it felt like she was more interested in fooling around than he was. She experimentally nibbled his earlobe, which she had heard drives guys wild. He tilted his head away from her and told her he was thinking about getting his ear pierced.

"You'll look like a fruit," she said and instantly regretted it. Billy Idol wore earrings, and she sounded like the idiots at her school who believed piercing your right ear meant you were gay ("The right ear is wrong, and the left ear is right").

Stefan said, "I know this guy who can walk down the street and get turned on by the girls he sees and by the guys he sees. What do you think about that?"

Veronika didn't know what to say. Homosexuality wasn't something she had ever really thought about. The Catholic Church said it was wrong, but they said a lot of stupid things, and her mom wasn't religious. They only went to church at Christmas and Easter.

"Do you hate fags?" Stefan persisted.

"Live and let live, I guess." Veronika thought about her mother's male friends, the ones who owned antique stores. "I don't like it when guys talk in that bitchy way, though." They sounded so phony.

"I know what you mean," Stefan quipped in a high-pitched voice, draping his wrist down.

Veronika made a face, even though she knew he was joking. Her spell had brought them together but didn't seem to be binding them. "I should let you go home," she said.

"I'll call you," he said.

Weeks went by and he didn't call. She remembered him saying relationships were a prison and wondered if that was why. Or maybe he knew lots of girls in Toronto and thought she lived too far away?

Maybe it was perfect the way it was: one night. She imagined herself taking drags on a cigarette and describing to a group of wide-eyed girls the cute boy she made out with in a graveyard and how she got into so much trouble. Except of course she didn't have any friends to impress. Would Sharon be impressed?

When Veronika got to the mall, Sharon was shuttering the entrance to the tobacco store. She was dressed all in blue (faded jeans, jean jacket, navy Keds sneakers), and a new perm had transformed her from a Winter brother into a Wilson sister. Veronika seized on her hairstyle as a conversation opener. "Wow, you changed your hair."

Sharon twisted the key in the lock before turning around with a blank look.

"It's very dramatic," Veronika added. She couldn't decide whether it was an improvement.

Sharon didn't say anything. Stood with her arms at her sides, her face impossible to read, like looking into a bowl of dry ice, waiting for Veronika to explain what she wanted.

"Want to go for a smoke?"

"Okay."

Instead of heading to the food court, Sharon brought Veronika to her car, a green Chevette in the middle of a rapidly emptying parking lot. They got into the car and took their cigarettes out of their purses (Sharon had a black leather purse with a raccoon tail) and lit up (Sharon had a cool silver box-shaped lighter, a Zippo she explained to Veronika, demonstrating how it worked). They smoked with the windows down and Led Zeppelin playing on the cassette deck. "I met this guy," Veronika began, and told Sharon what had happened without trying to impress her. Didn't try to piss her off either. Jettisoned the shield—provocation—she used to deal with people. "Why do you think Stefan hasn't called me?"

A grin skidded across Sharon's face. "Because he's homosexual?"

"Really? You think?" Veronika was shocked.

"You said he wore lipstick and didn't want to touch you."

Veronika let the idea slosh through her mind. Stefan was a punk, so the lipstick didn't necessarily mean anything, but the business about the "friend" who swung both ways might have been his way of telling her he was attracted to guys. That Stefan had rejected her because he was gay was certainly less insulting than the possibility he thought she wasn't cool or sexy enough. Sharon's take was interesting, as was the fact that she actually had one.

They started hanging out. The feeling of being bored that Veronika had with most people didn't happen with Sharon, no matter how much time they spent together. It was strange because it wasn't as though Sharon was super interesting. Or rather, it was hard to know if she was because she didn't talk much. Maybe the challenge of that was interesting?

One night Veronika invited Sharon over—they had never been to each other's houses, hanging out instead at the mall, in Sharon's car, at the group home where Perry lived. Tonight, Perry was away with his relatives, and Sharon stood at Veronika's door without moving.

"Come in, silly." Veronika gestured for Sharon to enter. "My mom and stepfather are out." Not necessarily together. Her stepfather was always at work, while her mom was likely with her friends, the men who owned antique stores.

The absence of parents didn't reassure Sharon, who glanced uneasily at the white carpet as she took off her sneakers. In sock feet, she slowly stared at the antiques that were everywhere. Veronika's mother worked as a picker, tooling around Southern Ontario in her husband's Jaguar to estate auctions in search of bargains to sell to dealers. Pieces she liked or couldn't sell accumulated throughout the house. Clearly, Sharon's home looked different, probably wasn't as fancy.

"My mom and I used to live in an apartment building," Veronika told Sharon, who didn't respond.

Veronika being out so much didn't go over well with her mother, who developed a stupid routine, an I'm-an-old-donkey-you-no-longer-love-but-there-is-nothing-to-be-done-about-it performance in which insecurity commingled with sarcasm. Theatrics Veronika found irritating. Her mother was so needy! Couldn't Erzsébet be pleased she had a friend? Admittedly a friend Veronika had never imagined for herself. Sharon was the opposite of popular; she had dropped out of school and worked at a mall, yet had that secret recipe for coolness certain popular boys did. She liked Sharon the way she liked those boys with their bashful grins—in spite of herself. When her new best friend could be bothered to have an opinion, it was usually to disagree with Veronika. Sharon thought white girls shouldn't date black guys (somehow the fact that her own boyfriend was Chippewa wasn't a contradiction); she'd never eaten pierogis, the best food ever, and wasn't willing to try them; and she thought punk music sucked and Led Zeppelin was the coolest band in the world. They were gods; Robert Plant was a fox.

Veronika skimmed her hand over the puff of Sharon's hair. "Is that why you got a perm? So you'd look like Robert Plant?"

Sharon moved out of reach. "You look like a Mennonite witch in those black dresses you're always wearing."

Veronika clicked the ash of her cigarette into a bottle cap with a dark-violet nail and cheerfully replied, "That's me, Mennonite witch!"

She knew her clothes didn't *really* bother Sharon; what Sharon hated was how different they were. Being friends with someone unlike you meant you might have to change or compromise. Veronika's big compromise was hanging out with Sharon's boyfriend, Perry. She hated that kids at school might think he was *her* boyfriend. He talked non-stop in a loud voice. Veronika thought Natives were supposed to be quiet, but Perry was a chatterbox. Today's topic was an unlikely scheme to make money that involved quitting school and going to Russia to sell designer jeans. When Sharon picked them up after school, she offered her two cents. "Yeah, because you know *so* much about exporting and retail." Exaggerated eye roll. "Stay in school, loser."

Though Sharon hadn't finished school, she didn't want Perry to quit. She wasn't older than him but acted like it, almost as though she were his mom, or a mama cat that has to swat her kitten to teach it to stay out of trouble. She had asked Veronika to write an essay for Perry. The assignment was easy; what was difficult was making it sound not that smart. She pulled it off, netting him a 70, and he asked her to do a book report.

She told him, "You have to write the first draft this time."

"Then I'd have to read the book."

"So?"

"So books are boring."

"So read a book that isn't boring. What are you interested in?"

He inhaled the joint they were sharing. "Drugs."

She grabbed the joint back. "We'll get you a book about drugs."

At the library, he was blown away that books existed that didn't have a "Just Say No" message. He wound up doing a book report on Carlos Castaneda's *Teachings of Don Juan*. While he didn't finish it, he was so enthusiastic about the chapters he did read that Veronika read it. This led to various conversations while stoned about religion and magic, and whether or not they should try acid (peyote not being readily available in Southwestern Ontario). Perry got hold of some LSD and did it twice in one weekend, which was enough to convince Veronika she wouldn't wind up crazy or dead if she dropped acid. Sharon was cool with trying it, too, or did a good job of pretending; it was hard to tell with her.

The three of them went into the woods to drop acid. Before getting out of the car, they each swallowed a blotter, a square of paper stamped with a ladybug. Perry led them along an overgrown path, and Veronika's arms got soaked from brushing up against wet bushes. Memory spilled—her father telling her about leaving Hungary in the middle of the night and walking through the forest into Austria, where he'd lived in a refugee camp while his parents visited different embassies, looking for countries willing to take immigrants. He was fifteen, a year younger than she was now. Kind of warped how different his life was from hers.

Was the acid working? She didn't feel that fucked up; she was just staring at things for long periods of time, the moss beneath her feet, a wet black leaf stuck to her hand. Sharon pointed to a birch tree. "Look at that tree."

"What about it?"

"It's neat."

"Yeah, it is." Veronika plunged into the soggy shrubbery to get to the tree. She could walk in a straight line without any problem; acid was supposed to be a hard drug, but being drunk felt harder. On acid, things were more interesting, that was all. Her fingers stroked the birch bark. The white skin of the tree didn't feel as smooth, as desirable, as she had imagined. She gripped a curled end and peeled it off.

She rejoined her friends, and they arrived at a tiny clearing facing a large pond. Sharon spread out her jean jacket as though it were a blanket and gestured to Veronika to join her. They lay on their backs on the floor of the forest, looking up at a sky the colour of old bones. Veronika felt dumb happiness envelop her as she inhaled the world, the rustle of cottonwood trees and damp, humid air.

Sharon popped gum into her mouth and chewed with her mouth open, releasing a cinnamon scent.

Did things taste different on acid? "Do you have any more gum?"

"Just A.B.C." Already Been Chewed. Sharon rolled over and pulled out her gum and put it into Veronika's mouth, feeding her as though she were a baby bird.

Veronika was so startled she didn't know what to say. If someone else had done it, she would have spat out the grey-pink wad, yelled, "Gross." Instead, the intimacy of the gesture felt like a weird privilege. Sharon had never hugged her, snuggled with her, or borrowed her clothes. Maybe the acid was making her act differently? Well, gum didn't taste different on acid. Being on acid was kind of boring; Perry had oversold the experience. Where had he gotten to, anyway? Oh, he was wading in the lake. They had been here once before when it was still warm enough to swim. The lake was on Chippewa territory, his territory, and Perry told them the water, though clean enough to drink, was so full of iron there were no fish. The water was a cloudy umber colour, and swimming in it had been like bathing in tea. Now, stepping into the water, Veronika gasped at how cold it was and almost slipped on the black twigs covering the bottom of the lake. She yelled to Perry, "What are you doing? It's freezing."

He didn't hear her. Lifting the hem of her dress, she waded over to him and repeated her question.

His jeans were rolled up above his knees, and his cuffs were drenched. "I'm looking for my 'power spot.'"

"Very funny," she said.

But he was serious, and, like the character in the Castaneda book, he couldn't seem to find it. This didn't discourage him. After Veronika led him back to shore, he crawled around, patting the earth. Upon reaching a promising place, he lay on his back with his hands over his heart, taking deep breaths. After a few minutes, he'd get up and move to another patch of pine needles and tree roots and start over. Sharon lit two cigarettes and handed one to Veronika.

"I feel less trippy now," Veronika said.

"Yeah," Sharon agreed. She put two fingers into her mouth and whistled for Perry, who emerged from the undergrowth.

"I saw a wolf," he told them excitedly.

"That's impossible," Veronika said. "We're too far south. Maybe you saw a coyote?"

"No," Perry explained. "It wasn't real. It was running across the clouds."

"Perry." Sharon's voice was suddenly stern. "How many tabs of acid did you take?"

Perry held up three fingers.

Acid went from boring to tedious. For two hours, Sharon and Veronika were half off, half on the drug while Perry tripped hard, his thoughts popping and frying. When it began to rain, they headed back to the car. The rain was so light it was more like a mist, but it took such a long time to get Perry moving steadily forward that Veronika was soaked when they reached the car. Her mind, at least, was clear of the drug, which could not be said of Perry, who was reverently stroking the car cushions.

"He can't go home," Sharon said. He'd be in trouble with the social workers if he showed up high at the group home.

"We can't go to my place because my mom's around." Veronika looked over at Sharon. "How about yours?"

"Nope," Sharon said. "We'll go to the Well."

The Well was an old rundown brick house where you could buy pot. A bunch of people lived there, including Goldilocks, Perry's dealer, a bear of a guy who was a bouncer at a strip club and had hair like Fabio. When they showed up, Sharon explained their situation, and Goldilocks obligingly opened the door to his bedroom and left for work. He wasn't put out by Sharon's request. In fact, he had looked grateful for the opportunity to do her a favour.

"He likes you," Perry said, echoing Veronika's impression. Sharon didn't respond.

"Let's fuck," Perry said. "It might make me come down."

Veronika expected Sharon to tell him to fuck off. Instead, she eyed the giant bed and said, "Okay."

What was Sharon's problem? Veronika was wet and cold and wanted to be chauffeured home. Instead, her chauffeur was bouncing around on the bed.

"Check it out! It's a waterbed."

Curious, Veronika sat on the edge of the swooshing bed. It was warm and enveloping. The water must be heated somehow. Sharon wriggled up to her and murmured in her ear, "Stay. This won't take long."

"Bite me," Veronika whispered back but couldn't summon the energy to get up. She was exhausted. *Maybe I'll crash for a bit.* She curled up on her side, her back to Sharon and Perry, who lay on top of each other a foot away from her. The noises they made while sucking face sounded like someone gently, repetitively mopping the floor. She buried her head in a pillow that smelled like aftershave and drifted off.

A different sound woke her up, an intake of breath travelling upwards like notes on a scale. It was Sharon getting turned on. Was Sharon that into Perry? Veronika had never gotten their relationship.

She peeked at them. Sharon was stripped to the waist, and Perry was touching her breasts, tiny barely there breasts with nipples like pink buds. They were beautiful; Sharon was beautiful. Veronika stuck her head back into the pillow, feeling more embarrassed than she had ever felt in her entire life. Her cheeks were hot. Should she stay and pretend it wasn't a big deal? Another glimpse at her friends increased her alarm. Perry was lying on his back with his jeans and underwear down, his dick jutting out, and Sharon was sucking him off.

Veronika crept towards the door. A feeling of being watched made her turn. Sharon was staring at her while stroking her boyfriend's dick. Giving Veronika a mute look that was a plea. *She wants me to help her.*

Before she could change her mind, Veronika dropped to her knees at the bottom of the bed. Sharon nudged Perry, who raised himself up on his elbows and grinned down at Veronika. "All right!"

The tip of his cock had a smear of transparent fluid that tasted salty, though within a minute of having him in her mouth she could taste only her own saliva. At first she tried to suck his entire dick, but keeping her mouth stretched that wide was uncomfortable, so she focused on the head. *Am I a slut?* Giving a blowjob didn't feel wild and bad; it felt boring and kind, as though she were doing him, and Sharon, a favour. A small hand stroked the top of her head; Sharon was encouraging her or reassuring her, Veronika couldn't tell. *I guess this is as close as two girls can get.* A short time later, Perry came in her mouth. Manfully, she swallowed a substance that was like hot mucus.

He sank back onto the bed. "Wow," he said. "That was freaky."

Veronika wiped her mouth with her hand. The slight pride she felt at her successful performance was eclipsed by embarrassment and confusion. She flung herself onto her back and closed her eyes. *Why did Sharon want me to do that?*

A hand caressed her belly, a soft hand, and Veronika's eyes fluttered open. Holy shit, Sharon was feeling her up. Veronika skittered away from her.

Sharon looked stricken. Then she reached wordlessly for her bra and T-shirt and put them on, her face blank. A blankness that was familiar, the poker face Sharon wore that until now Veronika hadn't realized was a poker face.

Perry, in a state of post-coital bliss, missed Sharon making a pass at Veronika. He cheerfully offered to "return the favour" but didn't protest when Veronika said she wanted to go home. While Sharon navigated traffic slowed down by rain and construction, Perry and Veronika discussed tripping.

"I didn't discover another world so much as I discovered this one," Veronika gushed. Led Zeppelin drowned out her observation; Sharon had cranked up the volume on the tape deck. They were stopped at a traffic light, and Veronika met Sharon's eyes in the rear-view mirror—they were tight with fury. *She hates me.* Shock went through her like ice. The light turned and Sharon redirected her attention to the road. Perry, meanwhile, started wailing along with "The Lemon Song" until Sharon told him to knock it off.

At home, lying in bed, Veronika realized she didn't think Sharon touching her was wrong, not really. It had just startled her. *Does this mean I want her to touch me?*

Maybe I do, maybe I don't. What she did know was that after twenty-four hours of not hearing from Sharon she was miserable. Not seeing Perry at school on Monday on the other hand was a relief. On Tuesday, she wasn't as lucky; she bumped into him at lunch on the front steps, having a smoke, and he delivered the unexpected news that Sharon had dumped him after they had dropped her off. Veronika tried to be comforting, even skipping her next class to hang out with him. Inwardly, she was stunned. *Is this because of me?* Perry didn't seem hurt about being dumped so much as pissed off. He also seemed interested in her, like Veronika could just replace Sharon and be his next girlfriend.

"I have to go to class," she told him when he suggested they toke up. But she didn't go to class; she marched over to Walpert Tobacconists.

"We need to talk," Veronika told Sharon, who regarded her stonily. Her boss, a large middle-aged guy, was sitting at the other end of the counter, thumbing through a pile of receipts. Elevator music seeped through an invisible sound system.

"I get off in an hour," Sharon said. "We can talk then."

They agreed to meet at the Orange Julius stand. When Sharon turned up, they headed to her car. Veronika told her she'd heard about the breakup, and Sharon said something about the relationship not working.

"Duh," Veronika said. She stood by the back door of the Chevette, waiting for Sharon to unlock it. They climbed into the back together, which was not something they ever did. Sharon stared out the window.

"Are we friends?" Veronika demanded.

Sharon didn't answer, refused to look at her.

"I wasn't trying to steal your boyfriend. I've never even given a blowjob before. I did it because I felt close to you."

That produced a scowl. "I don't feel close to you at all," Sharon snarled. Her hand clutched the door handle, and Veronika reached for her, and Sharon began to cry. Sobbed and gulped and wouldn't look at Veronika, who was flooded with tenderness. She slid her hands into the frizz of Sharon's hair, caressing her scalp the way she did when some kid she was babysitting freaked out. Lifted Sharon's hair from her face so they could see each other, really see each other.

"You're a lion," Veronika told her.

Then Sharon acted just like a creature from the jungle. She seized Veronika's shoulders and kissed her on the mouth, a kiss that was thrillingly hard. A kiss like she'd seen in the movies. A kiss she returned with tongue.

Sharon hesitated when Veronika suggested they go to her house.

"Don't worry. My mom's not going to think anything," Veronika said.

No one was home, which was better or maybe worse; Veronika was pretty sure she was about to have sex with another girl, and that was scary, even if it was with her best friend. As she put a Led Zeppelin cassette into her tape deck, it occurred to her that she and Sharon were rewinding the weekend, doing it over minus Perry, who never should have been part of the equation. Veronika pulled out the bedding, and she and Sharon got under the covers. Sharon gave her a goofy grin. It was the first time Veronika had seen her look happy. *Does she love me?* That felt like a terrifying responsibility.

They kissed for a long time. Then Sharon lifted Veronika's hands above her head and took off her T-shirt and bra. Veronika felt Sharon's mouth on her nipples. She hadn't realized having your breasts sucked could be sexual, that it wasn't just something babies did to their mothers. But she liked it. She liked it a lot, and when Sharon's leg fit between hers, she moaned. A knot of sensation pulsed between her legs, and she wanted to tell Sharon to do more but was afraid that if they talked about what they were doing, they would stop, that the spell they were under would break. Sharon removed the rest of Veronika's clothes. Being naked and having Sharon dressed was strangely exciting.

"I want to pop your cherry," Sharon said. "Can I pop your cherry?"

Veronika had no idea what this meant but nodded anyway. Felt fingers comb through her pubic hair and enter her, felt pain coat her pleasure, felt her vagina weep with fluid. It hurt and she cried out.

"I'm done." Sharon lifted up a knuckle covered in wetness, some of it blood, and she kissed the blood and thanked Veronika, who was freaked out.

What have I done? She got up and took fresh underwear out of her drawer and put her legs into the holes while feeling like a marionette. Sharon kissing her wetness was so intimate. Part of her felt like a precious doll while another part of her was terrified. *Am I gay?*

Sharon asked her if she was okay.

No.

"A cigarette," Veronika heard herself say. "I need a cigarette."

They went outside. Shared a cigarette on the porch steps as the sky darkened. The thick old trees were draining their leaves. Veronika had failed to rake them up this week, and they were everywhere, a cornucopia of colour. In front was a lone conifer, a tall ghostly tamarack that prevented her from seeing her mother until she greeted them.

Sharon shot up, words tumbling from her mouth; she hadn't realized how late it was, she had to get going, nice to see you again, Mrs. I'm-Sorry-I-Know-Your-Last-Name-Is-Different-from-Veronika's-But-I-Forget-What-It-Is.

When the green Chevette had whizzed off, Erzsébet remarked, "She's an odd friend for you."

Did her mother know what they had done? Panicky feelings enveloped Veronika like Pop Rocks going off in her chest. "What do you mean?"

Erzsébet hesitated. "Her mother's a prostitute."

That wasn't what Veronika was expecting. "She is? How do you know?"

"Everyone knows that. I'm surprised you don't."

Veronika shrugged as though it didn't matter, and in a way, it didn't. It would have yesterday or last week, but paled against the events of the afternoon.

Are we gay?

On the phone the next night, Sharon told Veronika she had quit her job and was moving to Sarnia; her cousin was getting her a better paying job in a factory.

"Sarnia! But that's no bigger than here!"

"Yeah, but I could get my own apartment. And you could...spend the night."

Be gay away from their mothers. Veronika was pretty sure that was what Sharon was asking. It was a question like all the other ones chalked across her brain she couldn't compute: Does sleeping with a girl count as losing your virginity? Should I fuck a guy? Am I gay? Is Sharon more gay than I am?

Veronika rerouted their conversation. "You should move to Toronto. It's way cooler."

"I don't like Toronto."

She didn't? Why hadn't she said so when Veronika was going on about how much she loved it? *She didn't want me to think badly of her.* She supposed that was also why Sharon had never said anything about her mother being a prostitute.

"Toronto's really cool," Veronika repeated to an unconvinced Sharon, who moved to Sarnia two days later.

They hugged goodbye at the bus station, Sharon clinging to Veronika with a desperate grip. Veronika was touched, and, to her surprise, turned on. Holding Sharon felt so perfect, but they let each other go.

Three weeks later, Veronika moved to Toronto because her mother's marriage blew up. She missed the occasion of her stepfather's pregnant girlfriend showing up at their house, but didn't miss Erzsébet screaming at him in Hungarian that he was a horse's dick whose semen had impregnated an ugly whore.

He had barely reacted. He was indifferent to her mother and to her. Though he'd been part of her life for nearly five years, he left it without any explanation, however pathetic. He didn't even bother to offer the standard bullshit line of "I'll be there for you even if your mother and I are no longer together." It was hurtful, insulting, yet Veronika couldn't work up much emotion. It was hard to get psyched out about divorce when you were worrying about whether or not you were gay. Plus, she'd already lost her real dad to cancer when she was a kid. This wasn't the same, not for her, not for her mother. Her stepfather had been chosen for them both like a couch at Sears—it was the best her mother could afford at the time.

Not that anyone would think that from the way Erzsébet carried on. Friends, relatives, a teller at the bank, the superintendent in their new apartment building, all heard about her divorce. Her mother seemed to relish sharing the details of her humiliation. Didn't Erzsébet have any pride?

Veronika couldn't take it. "He let you keep the Jaguar and the antiques, and he's giving you money every month for the next two years."

Erzsébet slapped her.

This had never happened before. Veronika was her darling.

Veronika rushed to her room and closed the door on

Erzsébet, who was already apologizing. Rubbed her stinging cheek and sobbed. Her mom was a bitch who had no idea about love. *I love Sharon.* But loving Sharon meant proving it, which meant having sex and being gay.

In Toronto, Veronika insisted on going to an alternative high school. There, her goth style, her taste in music, the fact that she was pretty and had done drugs meant she was inducted into the Cool Kids Pack, an experience that proved to be less satisfying than expected. She liked her new friends but didn't fall in love with any of them. Not with the six boys she fucked, not with the one girl she made out with when she was drunk. Yet, aside from a couple of awkward phone calls, she and Sharon didn't reconnect. Occasionally, she'd think about their last hug, prying open the memory like a locket and staring longingly before clicking it shut.

Weirdo-Freak

Nova Scotia, 1981

I was lying on my back on the side of the road while a girl and two boys in my sixth-grade class kicked me. As they booted my legs and thighs, they chanted "weirdo-freak" like it was a mantra. Since school started in September, my classmates had been hassling me, but until now it had been non-violent: paper airplanes downed into my curly hair, pencils knocked off my desk, my peanut butter and honey sandwiches on whole grain bread tossed into the garbage. It had sucked, but what sucked more was the fact that no one would help me. Not my teachers, who watched without comment, nor my parents, Quaker pacifists who advised me to ignore my tormentors.

Ignoring having my ass kicked was challenging. Still, I tried. With my eyes squeezed shut, I concentrated on the sound of the waves hitting the shore below, and imagined being a buoy, bobbing and floating on the sea. Tried to clear my mind of thought the way I did at Quaker meeting. *You are filled with lightness and air; you are letting go of worldly concerns.*

It didn't work. My heart skipped like a warped record, and I felt something press against my stomach. I opened my eyes—Kevin Slaunwhite was grinning down at me. Two of his teeth were missing; he was a Halloween pumpkin, holes carved out of him, face lit up and glowing with evil. He angled a muddy sneaker into my solar plexus, and I gasped with pain. Didn't horses refuse to trample the limp bodies of passive resisters? I was pretty sure that's what I'd learned in Sunday school when we had discussed Satyagraha. Unfortunately, Kevin and his pals weren't horses.

Kevin jeered, "Too chicken to fight back?"

"I'm not." Swaddled within my fear and humiliation was fury. Though I remained limp, I wanted to grab his ankle and jerk him to the ground.

Kevin took away his foot, and the others lifted my feet and my arms. They were swinging me back and forth, getting ready to toss me into the bushes, when my younger brother, Sun Berry, ran up to us.

"Leave her alone," he yelled.

The kids laughed.

"Buzz off," Kevin told my brother.

Sun Berry, who was recovering from a cold, cleared his throat and hawked a viscous gob of phlegm onto Kevin's face.

Kevin's eyes bulged with shock. "You little bastard!" He lunged at Sun Berry, who darted backwards, onto the road. A truck whizzed by, honking, and Sun Berry stood as still as a statue. Kevin backed away and walked down the road. It was, I supposed, beneath him to beat up a fourth-grader. Karen and Jimmy ran after their leader.

I stood up and looked for the items in my backpack that my classmates had thrown around. A brown paper bag that had contained my lunch was speared on a shrub, and I gently pulled the bag free. Sun Berry and I weren't allowed to pollute the environment and had to recycle as much as possible, flattening and reusing our lunch bags. The other kids had lunch boxes and readily discarded the saran wrap covering their bologna sandwiches on white bread, along with their empty potato chip bags and plastic pudding cups. Meanwhile, we got apples and bananas for dessert, the skins and cores of which we were expected to bring home for compost. This was why we got picked on—our family was different from everyone else in all of Nova Scotia.

Sun Berry and I walked home, trudging past bungalows and motorhomes.

"Why'd you just lie there?" Sun Berry asked me. "You're bigger than Karen. Why didn't you try and take her?"

Take her, I thought. Sun Berry talked like the other kids without having to think about it. Kids were always asking me why I used such long words. I'd try not to, but then I'd forget. Sun Berry grasped what needed to be done to blend in, and kids didn't give him as hard a time.

I explained I had been practicing passive resistance.

Sun Berry kicked a stone as though it were a soccer ball. "Kevin and them won't leave you alone until you fight."

I looked at him. "We're not allowed."

He shrugged.

We reached the duplex where we lived. Our landlady stared at us through the window without waving hello. She was old and didn't like us. She didn't have a husband because he had drowned in a storm. During the summertime, he had operated a motorboat shuttle service between the Cove and downtown Halifax. He had never learned to swim and hadn't been wearing a life jacket when he died.

I unlocked the front door and we headed upstairs. We could hear our parents fighting. My mother was always getting mad at my father's tone and calling him "passive-aggressive." Sometimes they acted like they were getting divorced. Other times, they'd neck in front of us and tell us to play outside because they wanted to have sex. They believed we should know about intercourse, and I couldn't remember not knowing about it. Copies of the *Kama Sutra* and *The Hite Report* were on the living room bookshelves.

"I'm going to the shore. Want to come?" Sun Berry asked. He loved the ocean and was agitating for a motorboat, but my parents said they destroyed ecosystems.

"Nah." I didn't feel like catching crabs or going rowing. I wanted to hide in my room and keep reading *Watership Down* to find out what happened next to the rabbits trying to escape the destruction of their warren.

My parents were engrossed in their argument.

"Fighting isn't Quakerly," I said in a loud voice. I was making a serious point, but they laughed. I went into my room. It was their fault I got picked on. Hugh and Elaine refused to give us normal lunches or go to a normal church, and they ran a health food store. They were excited about this book called *Seth Speaks* and spent every night doing transcendental meditation to channel the Bloomsbury Group, these dead people from England that did great things. I had learned not to talk about this stuff at school. For show and tell in third grade, I'd brought the little gold pyramids we kept around the house and tried to explain about pyramid power. Kids screamed "pyramid is stupid" at me for months. My parents acted as though being teased wasn't a big deal. The only person who tried to protect me was my younger brother, which was fairly pathetic.

I wrapped myself up in the orange and brown afghan my father had crocheted and picked up my book and tried to read. I couldn't concentrate. Someone, probably my father, had put on a Cat Stevens record. The words seeped in: It was a wild world and you couldn't get by on a smile. No, you couldn't. My father said it was bad to feel sorry for yourself, but shouldn't someone feel sorry for me?

On Saturday mornings, I helped my dad at the Lentil. A steady stream of customers came in while I opened boxes and put stuff away. The customers were Quakers and friends of my parents who went to protests, students who ate a lot of rice, rich women who bought crystals and astrology books, and seniors interested in vitamins and naturopathic remedies. "People talk about the generation gap, but it's really a question of where you're at," Hugh commented after a man who walked with a cane asked if we had a copy of *Psychodietetics*.

A woman set a yoghurt-making kit on the checkout counter, and Hugh, who was working the cash register, rang it up. While they discussed probiotic yoghurt, I spotted a guy shoving licorice chews into the pockets of his coat.

I yelled, "Dad, some guy is shoplifting!"

Hugh stepped out from behind the cash register and blocked the thief, who was dashing towards the door. Licorice packages fell from the man's pockets as he froze, trapped and unsure. Hugh picked up the candy and held it out to the man. "If you need it so badly, take it. If you can afford it, though, you should pay."

The thief looked startled and rushed out the door. My father returned to the cash register and calmly handed the woman her change.

"You shouldn't have confronted him," she told Hugh as she stuffed her yoghurt kit into a cloth bag. "You should call the cops."

"Clearly, you have more faith in the Man than I do," he said. He sounded mad. Mad at her when he hadn't been mad at the thief. I really didn't understand my dad sometimes. When the woman left, I asked Hugh why he hadn't called the police.

"They might file a report. That's about it."

I digested this. "So we let people get away with stealing?"

Hugh shrugged. "You could look at it that way."

If I let people beat me up, they will, I thought. If one person was good, but no one else was willing to be, wasn't it useless to be good? Quakers talked about non-violent resistance as though it were an act of courage, but when I tried to do it, I felt weak and ashamed. Ashamed because kids thought I was chicken when I wasn't.

"Dad, I don't want to go to the anti-nuke demo tomorrow."

"Why not?"

Now it was my turn to shrug.

Hugh refused to take me seriously. "You won't help make a sign tonight?"

Spray-painting old sheets with slogans and peace symbols was fun, but I wasn't giving in. "What if that guy who took the licorice tried to beat you up? Would you have let him?"

The smile on my dad's face disappeared. "I'm sorry he scared you. I was defusing the situation the best way I could."

"He didn't scare me," I muttered.

The next morning, I argued with both of my parents about going to the demo. I told them it was hypocritical of them to "force" me. Elaine said, "Don't be ridiculous. Get your sneakers on," and that had been that. The one thing for which I was grateful was the demonstration was downtown, so none of the kids around the Cove saw me holding up the dopey "Anti-Nuclear Family" sign. Demonstrating was embarrassing now that I wasn't a little kid who thought yelling in the streets was neat. Sometimes I agreed with the kids who picked on me: My family was weird.

While I was marching for unilateral disarmament, Karen, the girl who hated me, held a birthday party. The other girls in my class had been invited but not me. Someone had given her a gold locket, which she showed off at recess. An idea flowered in my head, a way to get back at her that was, technically speaking, non-violent. I marched up to her and grabbed the locket from around her neck. The chain broke in my hand and I let it fall to the ground.

In the afternoon, Karen and I were sent to the princi-pal's office. He was rubbing his temples because he was having a headache. He had a lot of them. He taught us gym, math, and science, but we'd had only one science class all year, in which he'd shown us the fuse box in the basement and described electricity. For math, he gave us textbooks and didn't show us how to do the exercises. Instead, he'd go to his office and read the newspaper. I did the work because it was boring to do nothing for three hours. Most kids didn't bother.

The principal asked me if I had stolen Karen's necklace.

I shook my head. "I didn't steal it; I broke it. And I broke it because she and her friends beat me up."

Karen interjected: "That was last week!"

The principal covered his eyes with his hands. We were hurting his head. "Okay, both of you stay in at recess tomorrow."

"That's not fair," Karen wailed.

He pointed at Karen. "You stay in at recess for the rest of the week, saucy boots!" He stood up. "Get back to math class."

We left.

"I hate you, weirdo-freak," Karen muttered.

"I hate you, saucy boots," I replied. I felt good. I couldn't believe how easy it had been to "take her." It made me wonder if I could "take" Kevin as well.

Walking home on the granite rocks that made up the shoreline was like clambering over giant eggs. I had to concentrate to make sure I didn't slip on the seaweed. Dimpled into the rocks were tiny tide pools where I caught crabs. I'd lean over the water and lift up rocks, carefully avoiding the sharp crusts of barnacles, and grasp a sidling crab, gently holding its pinchers closed so it wouldn't hurt me.

What if I caught Kevin? Found a way to hold his pinchers closed?

Sun Berry and I spied on Kevin. It wasn't difficult; he lived a few doors down from us and spent a lot of time playing road hockey outside his house. It was easier tracking him than it would have been for Kevin to spy on us, as we ranged further afield—the woods, the shore, the city. The challenge was getting him alone; he was always with his buddies. But early on Sunday, hours before we had to be at Quaker meeting, our opportunity came. We saw Kevin walking by himself carrying a hockey stick. We tore after him, my burlap bag of supplies in my hand.

"Kevin," Sun Berry called out.

He turned around.

My brother, who was panting, took a breath and delivered his line. "Want to see something sexy?"

Kevin planted his hockey stick on the ground. "What?"

"A *Playboy* magazine we found in the woods," I said. The boys in my class were obsessed with *Playboy*. I pointed to a path leading into the forest. "It's that way." My heart pounded. Would this work? "You can't tell anyone."

Kevin nodded. "Okay, but fast because I got to play hockey."

I gave him a twisted grin, and we crossed the street. The sun hadn't yet burned off the fog, and everything around us was grey—the cloudy sky, the leaden trunks of trees, the paved road, the gnarled roots twisting across our path. When I thought we were far enough from the road, I signalled my brother and we tackled Kevin.

He wasn't expecting it. I wrenched his hockey stick from his hand and tossed it away. He punched me on the shoulder, and his fist felt like a rock. Sun Berry sat on Kevin, and I held him down and wound my skipping rope around his arms and torso. Kevin screamed, and it came out high and girlish. He was scared!

I knotted the rope as tightly as I could. Sun Berry put a kerchief over his mouth and tied it. I opened a bulk container of peanut butter, stuck a knife into it, and smeared it across Kevin's face. When I had imagined this, he had cowered with fear, and I had felt powerful. Now that I was doing it, I felt nervous. I had also fantasized about telling him what a bastard he was; instead, I was as silent as I was at meeting. Methodically, almost tenderly, I covered his face with raw chunky peanut butter. Despite my gentleness, he began to cry. He didn't make a lot of noise—he snuffled while tears dribbled down his cheeks.

Sun Berry and I looked at each other. Without a word, we stopped what we were doing. I put away the peanut butter, and my brother untied him. I worried he might try and beat us up; he didn't even yell. Just picked up his hockey stick and tramped out of the woods with us trailing along behind.

As we exited onto the road, Kevin's friends ran up to us.

"Where were you?" one of them asked, giving Sun Berry and me a weird look.

Kevin couldn't meet anybody's eyes. "Nowhere."

Jimmy pawed at the gunk still left on Kevin's face. "What have you got on you?"

I didn't wait for his answer. Instead, I grabbed Sun Berry's arm and we tore down the street to our house. We didn't go inside. We went around back and sat at the end of the wharf, staring at the dark water below.

"That wasn't very fun," my brother said.

"No," I agreed. "It wasn't." In *National Geographic*, there were pictures of tribespeople with spears dancing around fires. I'd thought I'd feel like them, gleeful, triumphant. Instead, I felt mean. I had punished Kevin, but punishing someone turned out to be almost as bad as being punished. Not as bad but almost as bad.

From the porch, Hugh yelled at us to get ready for meeting.

Femme Confidential

Toronto, 1992

The minute I stepped into the club, I knew I'd be back. It was a men's bar with a big dance floor, flashing lights stolen from service vehicles, and a sound system with a boom-boom I felt in my chest. The tables were oil drums painted black with the name of the club stenciled on in white, and there weren't many stools—the place was designed for cruising. It was completely unlike the dark, sporty lesbian bar I'd visited once, except for the fact that tonight the place was full of gay women. The campy flyer Veronika had handed me a week earlier had a black silhouette of a woman in a cat costume, and the in-your-face name of the club night—Sex Kittens into Pussy—made me smile. One of the city's few female deejays was spinning. I hadn't realized she was gay, but seeing her here I recast her androgyny as queer instead of punk, or, rather, both.

I hadn't hung out with Veronika in a couple of years, not since the night she disappeared after we had sex. While I was moping over her vanishing act, I had met a boy named David, who worked at an antique store at the end of Queen Street West. In the shop, I had picked up a Magic 8 Ball and silently asked it if Veronika would come back into my life. A few shakes and I was unhelpfully informed: "Better not tell you now."

"How much is the Magic Eight Ball?" I asked the boy behind the counter, and he said a buck like it was a question, like if the amount were too high he'd give it to me for a quarter. I bought it, and he asked if I wanted to get Vietnamese food with him.

I blinked. Noticed he was slim and cute with long dark hair and a face somewhere between handsome and pretty. Noticed he was wearing a kilt.

Over bowls of pho, David told me he remembered seeing me at the store with Veronika. He'd thought we were lesbians.

"Really? Why?"

"You only paid attention to each other."

"You mean we didn't pay attention to you?" I teased.

He blushed. "I'm not that kind of a jerk. I've never even asked a girl I don't know on a date before."

Our date never ended. He came back to my house and moved in three months later when my roommate abruptly departed. She was an ex-addict, and one night after work, a guy on the street offered her some crack and she did it. She told me about it right away, accepted her reimmersion into addiction with a calm fatalism. I said, "I feel like I should organize an intervention." She laughed and hugged me, even though we weren't close. I never saw her again.

Everyone thought my boyfriend was gay; he worked for a gay male couple and sometimes partied with them at gay bars and had this slinky way of moving and touching things. But he wasn't gay; he loved going down on me. He didn't like me to go down on him; he didn't even like to fuck. What he liked was for me to use his cock like a sex toy, to rub it against myself because that way we'd come at the same time. Sex with him was easier than it had been with any other guy because everything I didn't want to do he didn't want to do. The only problem was all my sexual fantasies were about girls. I figured I must be bi, and that the fantasies were a case of the grass being greener on the other side, that if I had a girlfriend, I'd fantasize a lot about boys.

David encouraged me to explore, to sleep with women, and not in a sleazy I-can't-wait-to-watch way. He said he believed in sexual freedom, that no one person could meet all of another person's needs. Nonetheless, I was surprised when he acted on our principles. While I was at home with my family over the holidays, he slept with a woman he met at a New Year's Eve party and told me about it on the phone the day after. I wasn't prepared for the sharp, shocking pain. I sobbed into the phone, and he was alarmed. "I won't do it again," he promised. A promise I didn't ask for but didn't refuse, gripped as I was by pythons of jealousy and insecurity.

Perhaps we should have asked for advice from my parents, who had an open marriage. My mom had had the same boyfriend for years. Yet I didn't confide in them. I was pretty sure of what they would say, that it wouldn't be helpful. Hugh would tell me my jealousy was temporal, to observe it and then breathe deeply and release it. In his world, thoughts and ideas trumped feelings.

When I showed David the flyer Veronika gave me, he asked if I wanted to sleep with a girl so we would be on equal footing.

I shrugged. Wanting to go to Sex Kittens into Pussy had nothing to do with him. I wondered if Veronika had recently moved into Parkdale. After not seeing her for years,

I'd seen her twice in the past month. The first time was at the store where David worked. I was sitting behind the counter with him when Veronika entered with a petite older woman who resembled her, her mother presumably. Their conversation included a few words in a language I didn't recognize, and I remembered Veronika telling me she was Hungarian. I caught Veronika's eye, but neither of us said hello. Instead, she said something to her mother and they left.

Then last week we had run into each other at Coupe Bizzarre, a hair salon on Queen West for punks and goths and alternative kids. I waited for the hairdresser to finish with his client, whom I realized was Veronika. Her hair had been cropped into a black bob with crimson and lemon strands, shocks of colour like a red-winged blackbird. While he held the mirror up to the back and sides of her head, she explained she didn't have cash to tip him but hoped some shrooms would do and thrust a little plastic baggie into his hand.

"Liberty," she cried out, all phony-friendly, when she spotted me. "I haven't seen you in forever."

This wasn't technically true, but I didn't correct her. Her eyes assessed me: a skinny girl with glasses and long, curly hair wearing tapered black jeans and a Patti Smith T-shirt. I must've passed some test, because she rummaged through her handbag (the same black rubber porcupine thing she had when I first met her) and shoved a flyer at me. "I'm performing next week. You should come."

Now I was at the club and didn't see Veronika anywhere. Was I too early? Making my way to the bar through cliques of girls who looked like boys, I felt shy and ordered two beers.

I had almost finished my second drink when a woman offered to buy me a third. Out of a mixture of politeness and poverty, I accepted. We companionably clinked our bottles together. She was taller than me with a long-short hockey hairdo. Her voice reminded me of a slow motor grinding down, and I wondered if she was high. She told me, "I was at the airport and this guy bought me beers. I would have fucked him."

"You're not gay?" I asked.

She looked at me like I was stupid. "I'm gay. Why? Are you straight?"

"No, I'm bi."

"You have a boyfriend?"

I nodded.

"Does he know you're here?"

"Yeah, of course." As I said it, I realized my situation might not be typical. "We have an open relationship."

She slowly waved her finger in my face. "I'm not fucking your boyfriend!"

Bitchy thoughts flew into my head: *Uh, who asked you to? Uh, like he'd fuck you.* Veronika rescued me.

"Sorry we're late." Accompanying Veronika was a mixed-race girl who reminded me of the Hawaiian Barbie doll my politically conscious parents had given me when I was a kid: long, shiny black hair and big brown eyes with perfectly applied dark eye makeup. From the neck down, she was the antithesis of Barbie: chubby with a big heart-shaped ass that strained her black track pants.

Veronika gestured to her friend. "Do you know Holly?"

I was about to ask how I could possibly know her when I realized she was familiar. Two nights earlier, she had stood in front of me at the grocery store, trying to calm down a shrieking little boy. "Do you live in Parkdale and have a kid?"

She nodded. "Yup."

Veronika gestured towards the stranger who had bought me a drink. "Who's your friend?"

"Um." I didn't know the woman's name.

Holly giggled, and Hockey Hair, emboldened by the attention, introduced herself as Shawna. She asked Holly, "What are you?"

A look somewhere between bored and annoyed appeared on Holly's face. "Human."

Shawna continued, "I like Arabs."

Veronika elbowed Holly. "Did you hear that? She likes Arabs."

"Maybe she should find one." Holly took a slug of her beer and scowled at Shawna until she stumbled off.

At first, I'd thought Shawna had been asking Holly if she was gay. That was what I wondered about Holly, whom I assumed was black. In Nova Scotia, there were a lot of white-looking black people with a Scottish or Irish grandparent or two, and she looked like them. Did Holly consider the question about her background offensive, or the way it was phrased, as though she were a breed of dog, or the fact that it was Shawna's first question? I didn't have the guts to ask.

Veronika announced she had to go backstage. Holly and

I stood together, drinking our beer. I told her I liked her hoop earrings, that polka dots were an underrated print.

"Thanks. I got them at this store in Parkdale, Curious."

"Really? My boyfriend works there."

She looked at me with interest for the first time. "The guy in the kilt?"

"That's him." Kilts were his shtick; he even wore them during the winter, adding long johns to his ensemble.

"He's very cute. I always thought he was gay. I thought everyone who worked there was gay." Holly looked at me speculatively.

"Yeah, people always get it wrong. They think he's gay and I'm straight." I couldn't keep an edge out of my voice. It bugged me the way people assumed I was a deluded straight chick with a boyfriend who was gay, that no one ever considered I might be the gay one.

Holly nudged me. "Our girl's up."

A spotlight on the dance floor illuminated Veronika, who was nearly naked in a black and red merry widow with garters, stockings, and combat boots. It struck me anew how tiny she was. She had such a forceful personality that it came as a surprise that she wasn't built like a burlesque queen, that she had this hard, skinny little body she shook to the beat with jerky movements, dropping to the floor and springing up—hip hop on coke. With robotic locomotion, she pulled her bra away for a glimpse of bare nipple. Her speediness focused the audience, glued our eyes as we waited for the next few seconds when she'd flash her boobs. She was totally unselfconscious. Before departing, she peeked over her shoulder and rewarded us with a wiggle of her ass.

I felt like part of the A-list when she strutted over to us in her lingerie. A woman next to Holly presented her bar stool to Veronika, who made herself comfortable. Veronika pointed out a slender boyish creature with an aggressive hunch to her shoulders. "There's the bad girl everyone wants to fuck."

Holly added her two cents. "She's the bad girl everyone *has* fucked."

"She hasn't taken *me* home yet," Veronika whined.

I looked from Holly to Veronika. Clearly, neither of them was straight. How exactly had Veronika gone from het chick refusing drinks from dykes to big lesbo? And why did I feel like I had been left behind, had flunked a grade while she had skipped two?

The bartender came over with freebies from a woman too shy to approach Veronika directly, a round of shots. As we gulped them down, the-bad-girl-everyone-wants-to-fuck appeared. Wordlessly, she held out her hand to Veronika, who allowed herself to be tugged away.

Holly and I exchanged raised eyebrows. She was close enough to me that I could smell what I was pretty sure was Tommy Girl perfume. I wondered if I should make a play for her. I had never kissed a black girl before—or a black boy for that matter.

I bought her a drink, and she kissed me in the bathroom. She was a great kisser. Possibly the best kisser I'd ever kissed, except after necking for ten minutes in a bathroom stall I realized I wasn't into her. Did I want to fuck girls? Was it just an idea I had that didn't work in reality?

Holly took my fingers out of her hair. "I'm wearing a wig," she whispered.

I felt stupid. The only people I could think of who wore wigs were either drag queens or women going through chemo. Were wigs a black girl thing and I didn't know about it?

Bang, bang-bang-bang. Somebody was slamming her fists on the door of the stall we were in and telling us to get the hell out. I unlocked the door, and a woman glared at us. Holly smoothed down her top, and some girls who were standing in line for the toilets snickered. I was ready to bolt, but Holly was unconcerned—she made me wait while she reapplied her lipstick.

On Monday morning, after leaving my apartment to get a carton of milk for coffee, I spotted Veronika waiting for the streetcar. In tall boots with a sedate white skirt peeking below a fawn coat, she was likely headed to an office job, except I couldn't see her filing or doing secretarial work. She didn't seem the type to do routine work or be under some guy's thumb.

Veronika saw me staring at her. "Liberty," she yelled, waving frantically. When I went over, she began describing her encounter with the-bad-girl-everyone-wants-to-fuck. "Oh my God! What a disaster! Especially considering it started out so well. She totally took charge, which was awesome, because, Liberty"—clasp of my arm here—"you wouldn't be-lieve how many butches are really shy. But not her! She threw me down and fucked me with this huge dildo!"

A dildo? I tried not to be shocked. "Aren't dildos kind of pathetic?"

"Are you kidding me? They're hot!"

I couldn't believe she was telling me this story in public. I nervously glanced at the other people waiting for the streetcar, but they weren't paying attention. This was fortunate, as yet more intimate details flowed from Veronika: "She was riding me from behind, and I was totally wet and about to get off when she put her hands around my neck."

She mimed being strangled.

I frowned. "She hurt you?"

"Are you kidding? I didn't give her a chance. I bucked her off me, and she was all, 'Why'd you stop?' And I'm, like, 'Because S&M is something you discuss first.' I was going to put on my clothes and leave, except she had this loft bed, and I was so drunk I was afraid to climb down the ladder. I was sure I'd break my leg or something, so I just passed out."

My mouth dropped open. I didn't know what to say. I didn't have any comparable experiences. "Are you going to see her again?"

"Probably. We didn't have sex the next morning, but she made me breakfast and has been calling daily. The thing is, she's boring, so I've been trying to arrange a date to cut out the phone conversations about what we watch on television."

The scrape of the braking streetcar made us look up. While people stepped onto the car, Veronika madly scavenged through her spiked rubber handbag for the fare. I took a token from my wallet and handed it to her.

"Where are you working?" I asked.

"Property manager of an apartment building." As she clambered onto the streetcar, she put an imaginary phone to her ear: Call me! This, though I didn't even have her number.

Heading home to my boyfriend, I realized I was jealous. Not because I wanted Veronika or the bad girl, let alone scenes involving erotic asphyxiation. No, what I wanted was simpler: the wetness she had described.

On Saturday, I was back at the gay club, drinking with Veronika, who had called me. Neither of us was listed in the phone book, but she had dropped by Curious and asked David for our number, and he had given it to her. "She seemed sweet," he said, sounding surprised since I'd portrayed her as the bitch that hurt me. What was more surprising was he wasn't entirely wrong. The anger Veronika used to emit like a smoke machine had dissipated. Now she was a happy lesbian sex kitten.

Sex Kittens into Pussy happened only once a month, so the bar was full of men, and the deejay was playing dance music. No forays into college radio but an extra helping of deep house. I tried unsuccessfully to let the smooth incessant beat relax my brain. Holly was supposed to meet us at midnight, and I wasn't sure whether we were having a date or if I wanted it to be a date. After fooling around in the bathroom the other night, we'd headed back to Parkdale. Holly had repeated her earlier remark about my boyfriend being cute, and I wondered if she wanted us to have a threesome, something I'd always wanted to experience. Now that the possibility dangled before me, I realized I just wanted sex with a woman.

David said it was cool with him if I slept with Holly, but I wasn't so sure he was being honest. Before I headed over to the bar, we had a weird exchange. He'd said, "Remember the woman I slept with on New Year's Eve?"

"Obviously," I replied.

He ignored my sarcasm. "Well, she was transsexual." This was unexpected, both the fact of it and that he hadn't told me.

"So you're gay after all?"

"No!" he yelled.

He'd slept with a woman; she had a vagina, breasts; didn't I get that? He sounded angry. He was usually Mr. Laid Back, and it made me wonder if he was upset about Holly.

There was a special on draft, and I ordered one pint after another while Veronika devoured gin and tonics with lime. Even though it was chilly, she was wearing leather shorts with fishnets underneath. Her black and red hair was held back with bobby pins, and rhinestone earrings dangled from her ears. Was it superficial of me to want to be her friend because I loved looking at her? I wasn't alone. The gay men around us complimented Veronika's nineteen-forties-cigarette-girl-cum-punk look. She had an easy rapport with them, perhaps because her clothes and emphatic speech and gestures were as flamboyant as any drag queen. They kept trilling "girl" at her.

From the corner of my eye, I caught sight of the woman Veronika had gone home with. She was making out with someone.

Veronika's hand flew to her mouth when I pointed them out. Almost on cue, the-bad-girl-everyone-wants-to-fuck glanced over her shoulder and spotted us. She didn't look overly concerned.

"I...I don't understand," Veronika sputtered. "What should I do?"

I gripped her shoulders. "Tell her, 'Bitch, you're coming home with me.'"

"Seriously?"

"Uh, no."

Her eyebrows dived into each other. "This is bullshit!"

I agreed. "What you should do is ignore her because she's an asshole."

Veronika ignored me instead. She beckoned the bad girl with a sweep of her fingers, and the bad girl swaggered over to us.

"Are you planning to go home with me or her?" Veronika demanded.

The bad girl looked back at the girl she had been kissing and met Veronika's eyes without a trace of embarrassment. "Both?"

"Are you kidding me?" Veronika shrieked. Her eyes flicked over to the other girl, who was pudgy and dressed in ladies' acid wash jeans. "She's not even attractive."

The bad girl looked stunned. With blotchy cheeks, she hustled back to Ms. Acid Wash.

I couldn't believe Veronika. She was like Wonder Woman, lifting up bulletproof bracelets to a bolt of humiliation and coolly zapping it back.

"Can you explain what just happened?" Veronika asked me.

I couldn't begin to explain. There was no way I could have been as cool as Veronika, who didn't seem to get hurt as easily as I did. Nonetheless, I took the last bill out of my wallet and set it on the bar and offered to buy the next round of drinks.

"Would you have had a threesome if the other girl were cuter?" I asked.

Veronika dismissively waved her hand. "Threesomes are usually a combination of cheating and charity." She paused to reconsider. "Maybe if the other girl had been butch."

What was this butch thing? I didn't understand the appeal of the bad girl, who I guessed was butch. I thought she was a macho jerk.

Our drinks arrived. I took a sip of beer and felt it flame through my esophagus and wondered if I'd overdone it. The drinking I'd been doing was a strategic rather than hedonistic exercise. If I was wasted, I couldn't be expected to fuck Holly when she finally showed up. On the other hand, I didn't want to pass out on the floor. Veronika had had as much to drink as me but seemed sober.

"What's going on with you and Holly?" she asked.

I put my hand on the bar to steady myself. "I think she's really cool. We're both bi, and she doesn't care that I have a boyfriend."

"But? I hear a 'but' in there."

Sometimes I wished I smoked. "I feel like her friend."

Veronika wiped her forehead exaggeratedly. "Phew!"

"Huh?" She had lost me.

"This woman Maria picked her up last night at the Rose."

"Oh." I didn't know how to respond or even how to feel. I had thought it would be different with women, that we'd understand each other, but so far my experiences had been like a heap of pick-up sticks cascading down with the slightest move.

Veronika sighed. "You're going after the wrong kind of girl."

"What do you mean?"

"You need a butch."

A butch? I didn't want a butch. They were real dykes who'd judge a girl like me who had a boyfriend. Plus, not to be rude, but that type of woman wasn't my idea of hot!

"I want a pretty girlfriend!" I wailed. Was that what I wanted? A girlfriend? Yeah, it was. I wanted what I fantasized about, what Veronika probably had: lots of passionate sex with a woman.

Veronika pushed my shoulder. "Butches can be pretty! It's not about how long your hair is. You know the expression 'opposites attract'? Well, it's the same in dyke world. We're hot for what we're not."

I had felt genuinely attracted to Veronika but was too embarrassed to use this as an argument. Instead, I said, "Maybe I'm butch."

Veronika shook her head. "Trust me, you're not."

"I'm a line cook. I work with a bunch of guys," I offered. As I said this, I considered my fondness for *Vogue* and searching thrift stores for black velvet skirts. Even I knew that wasn't terribly butch.

"Why?"

The thread of our conversation had left me. "Why what?"

"Why do you work as a line cook? Why aren't you a waitress?"

I'd waitressed once back in Halifax. You had to be attractive. With my glasses and beaky nose and wild hair, I
wasn't classically pretty, but being skinny with good pro-
portions had been enough to get me hired at a popular
pub downtown. The tips were good, but I couldn't hack
men calling me honey. I didn't know how to toss off a joke
that would make them back off while allowing them to
save face. Instead, I'd seethe and fantasize about pinging
croutons at them. I told Veronika, "I don't like guys hitting
on me."

"But you don't feel like a guy?"

I shook my head. Burped and tasted a mouthful of
beer. Launched myself in the direction of an exit sign and
heard someone yell that I couldn't use the fire door. I had
already pushed it open and was vomiting over the side of
the railing. When I finished, I looked around for something
to wipe my mouth with. Leaves from a nearby tree worked.
I cradled my head, which buzzed with pain. Veronika came
out, shivering in her shorts and waving some bills in my
face. Cab fare. We had become friends, I supposed.

In the cab, I realized I was going to break up with David
when I got home. I wanted to expel myself from the relationship with the abrupt urgency with which I had thrown
up my beer. I wanted to know if I was gay, and I couldn't
figure that out with a boyfriend.

At our apartment, I spotted two empty bottles of wine
on the counter. Bottles I knew David had drunk. He did
this sometimes, and I didn't like it. Tonight I didn't mind.

It's easier to dump your lover when you're feeling annoyed with them.

David was passed out on the futon couch in the living room, still in his kilt. I told myself I should put a blanket over him and go to bed and have the discussion in the morning. Instead, I shook him awake and was treated to sour wine breath.

"David," I spoke sharply.

His eyes fluttered open. "Why are you looking at me like that?"

"Like what?"

"Like I've been diagnosed with cancer."

What I needed to say floated around in my head, alphabet noodles in a pot of soup.

He reached for his cigarettes. Lit one and took a drag. "Seriously, what's up?" His eyes were worried.

I sat on the floor with my arms wrapped around my knees. "I want to break up. I think I'm a lesbian."

He laughed in a rough way, and I wondered if he was still drunk. "That's funny. That's really funny because, you know, I think I might be a lesbian, and for the last six months I've been wondering how to tell you."

I had no idea what he was talking about. "What's that supposed to mean?"

David took another drag on his cigarette and explained. The reason he'd had sex with the transsexual woman was to talk to her, to tell someone what he wanted to do, which was live as a woman. "I wanted to see her body, see how real it was possible to be."

"God," I said. My voice was shrill and high, and I hated the sound of it.

"Are you that surprised?" he asked.

"Kind of, yeah." What he was saying explained a couple of things—his femininity that got mistaken for gayness, and how not having sexual intercourse was a non-issue—but I was still surprised.

"Part of me has been thinking about this forever." The bottom of his cigarette crinkled with wires of light, and he told me stuff I'd heard before that meant something different now. The time he'd put on his babysitter's lipstick, the misery he felt when a carpet of hair appeared on his chest. "I can't explain it rationally, but it is totally depressing not to have boobs, not to have a vagina."

"Are you going to get a sex change?"

He sighed. Butted out his cigarette. "I don't know. Bottom surgery is scary. Things didn't work so well in that department for the woman I slept with. She says she still can't pee right. I thought I'd start with hormones."

I stared at the ceiling. David wanted to have a vagina. Why hadn't he talked to me about this? It was crummy that he hadn't. Then I remembered how in high school I had thought about telling my brother I was attracted to girls and didn't because I'd been scared he might get drunk and accidentally blab my secret. Now that seemed paranoid and stupid.

David asked, "Are you mad?"

I shook my head. Got up and sat on the couch beside him. Felt him cradle my hand.

"Would you call me Dana?"

He already had a name picked out.

"Okay." I said his new name out loud. "Dana."

David—Dana...I was going to have to start thinking of

her as Dana, as she—wiped at one of her eyes. "I'm so glad you're okay with this. I didn't think you would be. That's why I didn't tell you."

Tears formed in my eyes. "Yeah, but it's sad we're breaking up."

Dana stared at me. "Being with me if I transition means being a lesbian."

Right, okay, why hadn't I thought of it that way? What she was saying was perfectly logical and didn't matter—I didn't want to be with him—her—anymore.

"That's not enough, is it?"

"No." I didn't try to explain. The truth I supposed was I hadn't meant to get involved with him. I had wanted Veronika and consoled myself with David.

She pulled her hand away from mine and stood up. "Fuck!"

I stood up. "David..."

She turned from me, threw up her hands, stormed into what had been our bedroom, and closed the door.

The Babysitter

Ontario, 1977

When David was eleven, his mother hired Karen, their babysitter, to come live with them for the summer, but when David's father stepped out of their truck, it was with a stranger, a girl in cut-offs who had dirty-blonde hair that hung down to her bottom. "This is Roxanne, Karen's cousin," his father said, nervously rubbing his beard.

"You smell like bubble gum," David told Roxanne.

"It's my lip gloss. I don't have any gum on me."

While David's parents went into the kitchen to talk, David and his younger sister, Dawn, showed Roxanne her room. They sat on the tiny bed and watched her unpack her suitcase. She took out rolled-up posters of a band and thumbtacked them to the wall. David stared. They were dressed like superheroes with tight pants and platform boots, and they had long hair and wore makeup.

"KISS is my favourite band," Roxanne said. She was holding a portable radio and fiddling with the dial, trying to get a station. A song came on, and she sang along. It seemed like she knew the lyrics to every song that played on her radio. David brought her his collection of eight-tracks, mostly K-tel compilations but also 10cc and Deep Purple.

"'Smoke on the Water' is my favourite song," he told her.

"'Beth' is mine," she said. "Peter Criss wrote it for his wife. Lucky woman." She dipped her finger into a tiny pot of pink lip gloss, and rubbed some on her lips. Her lip gloss *did* smell like Dubble Bubble gum. He hoped she would kiss him good night. This was going to be a great summer!

The next morning, David woke Roxanne, who said she wasn't used to getting up early and stumbled around. In the kitchen, his mother had made coffee and tea before leaving for her nursing class. David watched Roxanne uneasily eying the flies buzzing around the honey they took in their tea. There were strips of flypaper hanging from the ceiling like streamers, but they were already studded with dark, tiny corpses, unable to absorb more. Roxanne gagged at the sight and set down her tea: "I don't think I'll be drinking this."

David took her outside to help with the chores. They walked along a grass path, and Roxanne complained that her sneakers were getting soaked from the rain.

"It isn't rain, it's dew," David told her. "That's why I wear boots in the summer."

At the barn, he unlatched the double doors and stepped aside to let Roxanne in, then closed the doors behind them and opened a second door. "Airlock procedures," he said the way his dad always did.

As soon as the goats spotted them, they bleated like

sheep and charged up to the front of their stalls, the bells around their necks clanging. One of them tried to stick her head through the slats, her eyes eager and curious.

"They're like dogs," exclaimed Roxanne. "What are their names?"

"We don't name them," David said. Any animal they planned to kill didn't get a name. He added, "They're fainting goats."

"They faint?"

"Not really. Mostly they just freeze if something scares them. The kids sometimes fall over. It's pretty funny. But we're not allowed to make them do it."

David opened the first stall and put a rope around the neck of a goat with an enormous udder. He brought her to a low table, which she clumsily leapt up on. He put her neck through the head-catch to hold her head in place.

Roxanne said, "It looks like you're hurting her."

David shrugged. "She doesn't mind."

It was true. She was busy pooing. She had flicked her tail, and turds fell out of her bottom like gumballs from a machine. David sprinkled hay into a trough, and she gulped it down. While she ate, David placed a bucket underneath her udder and began to milk her.

"Have you ever milked a goat?" David asked Roxanne, knowing by the squeamish look on her face that she hadn't.

"No!"

"Want to try?"

Roxanne gamely crouched down, and David placed her hands on the goat's nipple and told her to push upwards, into the breast. Roxanne tried but nothing happened. "You made it look easy."

"Close the area around the nipple first."

This time, as Roxanne squeezed the nipple, a thin stream of liquid squirted out. She gripped the breast again, pressing up, and milk gushed out, landing on her jeans. She released the breast and stepped back. "Ugh."

David reached under the goat and effortlessly milked her. He had been doing this for almost three years.

Roxanne wiped up her jeans with hay. "That felt like giving a hand job!"

"What's a hand job?" David asked.

Roxanne's face went pink. "I shouldn't have said that."

That meant hand jobs had to do with penises and vaginas. Living on a farm, David knew about mating. "Does a hand job mean making babies?"

"No," Roxanne said. She looked like she wanted to explain but didn't say anything more.

Roxanne told David she thought milking goats was gross, so gross she barfed the second morning they did it. After that, he stopped waking her up early. In the afternoons, Roxanne helped them out, weeding the garden and feeding the chickens. The chickens had their own house with a yard surrounded by wire mesh. The yard was smeared white with their excrement.

Roxanne rubbed the sole of her sneaker on some grass. "I didn't know poo could be sticky."

David and Dawn threw food at the chickens, which fluttered about pecking the ground.

"Do you worry the chickens will get angry and peck

your eyes out?" Roxanne asked.

"The chickens like us," Dawn said.

"Yeah, but you kill them." Roxanne slid her hands into her back pockets. "Wait, your parents don't make you kill them, do they?"

David shook his head. "My mom kills them."

"That's weird."

"Not really." His mother had grown up Mennonite, where people still lived like they did on *Little House on the Prairie*, so of course she knew how to kill a chicken. She also wore long skirts she sewed herself. It had been a huge hassle to get her to stop making clothes for him and Dawn and order stuff from the Eaton's catalogue.

"I don't think your mom likes me," Roxanne continued.

"Yes, she does." As David said this, he realized it wasn't true. His mother didn't approve of Roxanne any more than she approved of him. He'd catch his mom watching him with this look, like she wasn't sure about him. He didn't understand it. He did his chores, got decent grades, and he wasn't mean. Roxanne wasn't mean either; she was the best babysitter they'd ever had. Why didn't his mother like her?

In the evenings, David and Dawn hung out in Roxanne's bedroom, where they all danced together. Roxanne taught them the Bus Stop and the Hustle, and Dawn tried to look like Roxanne by stuffing her flat chest with socks and tying the bottom of her shirt into a knot above her belly button. Other nights, they played cards: Fish, Crazy Eights, Cheat, and War. David got good at War and began to beat Roxanne at the face-offs. "Bull poop," she shrieked when she lost to him. David and Dawn giggled, and Roxanne explained she was being more polite than if she used the "S-word." She was so interesting, like a television show. She told them about drinking beer and driving dirt bikes and making out with boys.

"I probably shouldn't tell you about boys. Your mom would get mad," Roxanne said.

"Only if we told her," David pointed out.

Dawn jumped up and down on Roxanne's bed. "Tell us, Roxanne! Tell us!"

Roxanne shook her head. Pretended making God's eyes with yarn and Popsicle sticks required her full attention.

A brainwave hit David, who ran off and returned with Dawn's most prized possession, Froggie, a stuffed green frog. He opened the window and dangled Froggie by the edge of a webbed foot. Dawn was horrified and pulled at the back of David's shirt. "No, no, he'll die."

Roxanne got up. "You stinker!"

"Tell us," David insisted.

"All right, all right," she said. "Give your sister her toy."

David handed Froggie back to Dawn, who ran out of the room, clutching him, Roxanne following. He found them outside on the porch. Roxanne was braiding Dawn's hair. Something crawled across his guts—he wanted Roxanne to hold him and braid his hair. He felt so jealous of Dawn.

The next day in the hayloft, Roxanne was wearing a pair of white pants with lots of pockets, and she stuck out one of her legs and said, "These pants got me into trouble."

David was puzzled. "Your parents got mad at you for wearing tight pants?" They were snug, what the boys at school called "read my lips" jeans.

Roxanne laughed. "No, I got into trouble with some boys who pantsed me."

David plopped down on a hay bale beside Roxanne, and Dawn, who had been looking unsuccessfully for one of the barn cats, joined them.

"It was at school during lunch hour," Roxanne said. "I went into the woods to have a smoke with these guys. One of them, Stevie, didn't have any smokes left, so he tried to steal one off of me. I wouldn't give him any, and he pushed me down into the grass and got on top of me. Then he ordered his friends to take off my pants, and they did! Stevie wouldn't give them back to me for the whole lunch hour! Then he had the nerve to say, 'I like your pants.'"

David and Dawn bombarded Roxanne with questions. Did she like Stevie? Was he cute? Did the boys get into trouble? Roxanne blushed and said yes she liked Stevie; he looked like Scott Baio, who played Chachi, and the boys didn't get into trouble because she hadn't told on them.

That night in bed, David thought about the boys taking off Roxanne's pants. He imagined being the boy who lay on top of her. To make it more real, he rolled onto his stomach and rubbed up against the bed. He also imagined being Roxanne, having breasts that pushed up against the bed. It felt good and he kept rubbing. He must have made the top bunk jiggle too much, because Dawn suddenly kicked the mattress with her feet.

"Stop it!" Dawn yelled. "You're keeping me up."

"I'm not doing anything!" He felt like an old, sick dog he had once seen shit on a rug. It had slunk off. It had felt ashamed.

"I'm going to tell on you," Dawn sang.

David swung his head over the side of the bunk and watched his sister gleefully kick her feet in the air. Did she know what he'd been doing? Probably not, but she'd still guessed he was up to something bad.

He tore down the ladder of the bunk bed and leapt on Dawn, seizing her throat and choking her. She made a gurgling sound like she was going to barf, and David instantly let go. Dawn began to cry.

"I'm sorry, I'm sorry. I didn't mean to." David couldn't believe it. He had almost killed his sister.

"I hate you and so does Froggie," Dawn said. She pulled the covers over her head so she wouldn't have to look at him. The ladder squeaked as he made his way back into bed. He tried not to cry and wound up sniffling. It was the worst fight they had ever had.

At the end of the summer, the hay was baled. David and Dawn chased after the tractor while their dad and men and older boys from other farms tossed the bales into the back of a truck and loaded them onto the conveyor belt. David caught a baby snake. It had brown, red, and yellow stripes, a rippling ribbon of colour, and he showed it to Roxanne, who didn't even squeal. At the beginning of the summer, she would have. Then she'd almost fainted when she saw parts of a dead deer in the compost heap.

Before baling the hay, David had gone with his dad to look at a new baler. On the drive down, he asked why Mom didn't like Roxanne. His dad didn't answer at first. Then he said, "Girls like Roxanne, they're too mature for their age. They aren't much for school, they wear tight clothes, act sexy." He stopped. "Don't repeat what I said to your mother, okay?"

"I won't," David promised. He'd never had anything on his dad before and didn't like the feeling. He also didn't like his father calling Roxanne sexy.

After baling the hay, his dad made ice cream. While he cranked the handle, David and Dawn and Roxanne lay together under a quilt on the porch. David had his butt against Roxanne's belly, which felt round and hard and tight like the top of a drum. Roxanne was cradling him, and he kissed the inside of her wrist.

She whispered, "Guess you're not a fairy."

Being a fairy was bad, so it was good he wasn't one, except she took her hand away. He wanted to be her boyfriend and couldn't because he was too young.

The next morning, Roxanne left. David was pretty sure his mother had sent her away.

A few months later, he was standing at the top of a hill with his mother and sister, looking down at a cranberry bog brimming with berries. Everything was saturated with colour: black-green trees, a sky the shade of cinders, and a crimson carpet of berries. If it didn't rain, they would pick cranberries all day. He and Dawn were always picking berries: strawberries, raspberries, blueberries, blackberries, and, finally, cranberries. He asked his mother how fruit could grow in water. Everything else grew in dirt.

She replied, "You did."

"What do you mean?"

"When you were in my stomach, you were in a sac of fluid that protected you."

"Oh." David hadn't thought about the mechanics of pregnancy before. As he tugged the cranberries from their branches and listened to them plink into a metal milking container, he realized Roxanne was having a baby. That was why her stomach had felt so big and hard. It was bad to have a baby when you were a teenager, so his mother sent her away.

She'd left her lip gloss behind. David discovered it in what had been her room but became his because his parents decided he was old enough not to have to share with his little sister. At night, he would open the lip gloss and rub it on his lips like the members of KISS, and he would imagine kissing Roxanne and being kissed by her.

Good in Bed

Toronto, 1993

On a hot August night, I showed up at Grrl Spot, wearing very little clothing and hoping to find a woman who would remove what was left. I was wearing lingerie as outerwear, which can be done if you accessorize properly: My black velvet bra was accompanied by an onyx pendant, and my red silk boxer shorts that were a size too small and more like hot pants were paired with army boots. Some people might have called my look "genderfuck," except it wasn't really. Masculinity or even androgyny just wasn't me. I wanted butch and femme to be like shoes, something you could slip on or unlace, but it wasn't that simple.

I had come around to Veronika's way of thinking. After I split up with David/Dana, I dated other femmes, but nothing gelled. Approval at the sight of writers I admired on their bookshelves or vintage dresses in their closets didn't translate into passion. Any excitement I felt had more to do with the fact that I was touching breasts that weren't mine for the first time in months. Yet I didn't consider butches until I met Veronika's new girlfriend, Diamond. She had been a character in some hokey Canadian television show I hadn't seen, since I'd grown up without television, and had the flawless appearance of the professionally attractive. She was tall with killer cheekbones and dark hair that tumbled to her waist.

"Your girlfriend's so beautiful!" I exclaimed to Veronika. "I want to French braid her hair." We were in a club, and I had dropped some X and was a little too high. The pleasure whooshing through me was cut with static bursts of paranoia. "Don't tell her I said that! Promise!"

"Chill, I won't," Veronika said, though of course she did. "Diamond is B.D.H. Butch despite hair."

It was true that Diamond wasn't girly. I watched her imitate Veronika fixing her hair, and the mockery reminded me of straight guys cross-dressing on Halloween—they think it's a hoot, have no idea how to pull it off or how off their performance is. It was kind of endearing, and I developed a small crush on Diamond. Since she wasn't available, I began flirting and hooking up with other butches. Sex was a revelation, more thrilling and, paradoxically, more comfortable.

I didn't fall in love, though some girls fell hard for me. I wasn't like Veronika, who could get anyone she wanted; I was like an indie band or cult film that becomes an obsession for a few. One woman followed me home from work and left a seven-page letter in my mailbox; I had to tell her very firmly that was not cool. Another woman wove dozens of dandelions into my bicycle basket. I sensed with these women that, as in my relationship with Dana, I'd too easily dominate, and I wanted a more equal relationship. If I couldn't imagine spending the rest of my life with someone, I didn't see the point of continuing dating. Veronika thought this was the stupidest thing she'd ever heard, and Holly echoed her: "Girl, you're so serious!"

Grrl Spot was Veronika's first foray into organizing dyke nights. Men were allowed if they came with women, though few ever turned up. Fags had their fag hags, but dykes didn't really have the equivalent. The neighbourhood bar that hosted Grrl Spot was dark with low ceilings and patio lanterns strung along the walls. It was like an ongoing party in someone's basement. Different deejays played every week, and the music ranged between metal, industrial, hip hop, reggae, house, and drum and bass. Hardly anyone danced—frumpy couches took up most of the floor space.

On the night I showed up in my underwear, I planted myself on the last empty couch. Before long, a woman approached me.

"Excuse me, this sounds stupid, but don't I know you?"

A big handsome Portuguese woman with soulful brown eyes and pouty cheeks named Maria was standing in front of me. I told her, "You used to date my friend Holly."

"Right, Holly."

"And I've seen you around with lots of other women."

She ran a hand over her slicked-back hair and sighed wearily. "Yeah. My problem is I have sex with a girl and she falls for me. I'm too good in bed."

Well, she was full of herself! I batted my eyelashes and told her that if she was trying to impress me, it wasn't working. "I'd be more intrigued if you told me you were bad in bed. In fact, I'd feel compelled to prove you wrong."

She smiled, and I was relieved she had a sense of humour. "You're supposed to see through my rough exterior to my insecurities," she told me.

Another line, but this one was delivered with awkward irony: my turn to smile.

Maria ran a finger down my bare arm, and, although my skin was damp with sweat, I shivered. "Would you like me to get you a drink?" she asked.

"Sure, gin and tonic with lime."

At the bar, a white girl with a nose stud, a huge rugby shirt, and the same hairstyle as Veronika (long with two tiny, thin braids at the front) was taking orders. Grrl Spot was cool, maybe a little too cool. Meeting women, never mind getting laid, required effort, but tonight things were going my way.

Maria returned with my drink and joined me on the couch. Above us, a film projector played *Faster, Pussycat! Kill! Kill!* with the sound off. Maria placed her hand between us. I inched closer so she was touching my thigh. She asked me where I worked.

"At a diner, but I'm about to start an M.L.I.S."

"Say what?"

"A master's in library and information studies."

"Library. And. Information. Studies." She said the words one at a time as if she was trying to remember them and took her hand away from my thigh. "Does that mean you're going to check out my books?"

I tried not to bristle. "More like learn to do research and build databases."

"You must have to go to school for a long time." She said this in a strange way, like she was impressed and resentful.

"Depends what you consider a long time." My eyes met hers. "What do you do?"

"I work in a factory."

"That's cool."

"It's boring."

This was said in a pissed-off tone I didn't know how to respond to. I played with the ice in my drink while she lit up a cigarette. She watched a woman on the dance floor with short blonde hair move her hips to James Brown. I felt jealous. I didn't want to marry her, but I needed her to find me the sexiest woman in the bar.

"Do you want to go home with me?" Maria blurted out.

"Very much."

She kissed me, her tongue firmly positioned in my mouth. Not a subtle kiss, but I didn't care that much because I was really in the mood to have sex. When I moaned, she stopped and said, "My truck's out back."

The air against my skin felt like a sunburn. According to the news, the heat was breaking some kind of record. Maria opened the door of her truck for me. When I got in, I rolled down the window and wished for a breeze.

"We should drive by Holly's place," she said.

"Uh, that would be weird."

"Yeah, she might be sucking some guy's dick."

I looked at her. "What do you mean by that?"

She didn't answer. Focused on spinning her truck around and heading south to the expressway, which I supposed meant she was taking me to her place.

I repeated my question. "Why would you say that about Holly?"

"Because that's why we broke up."

They hadn't gone out long enough to have truly broken up—a couple of months. Holly had told me Maria was too controlling.

She continued, "I'm seeing her, okay. She's cute, she's

femme, she seems like she's part of the club. Then she gives a blowjob to some guy. It's not like we agreed to be serious or monogamous, but I don't want to hear shit like that." She made a face.

"Wouldn't it be just as bad if she had gone down on a girl?"

"It's different," Maria insisted. "I'm getting screwed over by some guy."

I didn't look at it the way she did. Maybe it was prejudiced, but I found men less of a threat than women. Sure, men had power and privilege and dicks, but they weren't as interesting as women. If a woman I was seeing preferred them or chose them because she thought it would make her life easier, I felt sorry for her. Admittedly, this hadn't come up for me as an issue, or at least not when there had been anything at stake.

"Do we have to talk about Holly?"

"Oh. Sorry. Hey, are you hungry?"

"Not really."

"So you want to go straight to my place?"

"Uh-huh." I watched Maria expertly shift from third gear to first, and her easy skill attracted me more than the obvious ways in which she was butch. "Are you nervous?"

"Yeah." She kept her eyes on the road ahead of her.

"We don't have to do anything if you don't want."

But when we got to her basement apartment, she was all action. Didn't even offer me a drink. Dimmed the living room lights and got on top of me and squeezed my breasts like they were fruit she was checking for bruises. I was wondering how to get her to slow down when she abruptly stood up.

"Excuse me," she said in a deep voice. She walked down the hall to what I guessed was her bedroom. I heard her rustling around in her drawers, and I had a sinking feeling she was putting on a strap-on dildo.

"You can come in," she called back to me.

I entered the room. No light had been turned on, though some light seeped in from the hall. Maria was sitting stiffly on the edge of the bed, and I put my hands on her shoulders and pushed her down. Hard rubber jabbed my thigh. I had been right about the dildo.

From her position beneath me, she asked in a shocked voice, "What do you think you're doing?"

I laughed. "Surely, you don't think being femme means I get into the missionary position while you fuck me with your dick and I scream like a porn star?"

Maria did not laugh.

Oh, it *was* what she thought. I took a deep breath. "Penetration is physically uncomfortable for me, painful. I don't even wear tampons." I didn't like putting this into words. So far, my female partners had mostly figured this out as we went along. I didn't like talking about it, though, because it made me feel inadequate, like I couldn't provide everything on the menu. It didn't help that no doctor had been able to explain why penetration hurt.

"I guess we can't have sex then," Maria said.

"What?" I shrieked. "Are you serious?" I suddenly realized that if I had been a lesbian back in the day, I would have joined the feminists who rebelled against the unreconstructed butches and femmes. For me, butch-femme was descriptive, not proscriptive.

"What can we do?"

"Kiss? Fool around?"

Maria removed her dildo and harness. Went over to a battered chest of drawers and shoved her equipment inside and rejoined me on the bed. She kissed me, and this time it didn't feel like she was trying to prove something. We slid our hands over each other's bodies, and she peeled off most of my clothes and some of hers. She was too shy to tell me what she liked; she would just nod slightly when I asked. She looked nervous when I sucked her nipples, even though I could feel they were erect. When she began breathing hard, I teasingly placed my fingers on the waistband of her boxers to slide them down. She immediately put her hand over mine, stopping me.

"Why?" she asked.

"I want to feel your naked body. I want to look at you."

"I've got kind of a beer gut happening."

"Maria, your body's fine." She was chubby in a lush well-proportioned way, and I liked it. Veronika liked women with slim boyish figures, but I didn't care so much about body type. It was more important that my sexual partners were wild with desire for me than that they looked a certain way.

Maria pulled off her boxers, folded them and set them on a chair, and crawled under the sheets with me. We kissed some more, and when she stopped, I looked into her eyes. Saw enjoyment entwined with apprehension.

She sighed. "I feel so girly. I never do this. Take off all my clothes, I mean, maybe once or twice. My ex-girlfriend lived with me here for two years, and she never saw me naked unless she walked in on me in the shower."

I was shocked. I had heard about these untouchables

but had never met one. Stone butch was this hard cool thing that was supposed to be about wanting to be a man, but for Maria it sounded depressingly like the same thing almost every woman I knew felt—I don't like my body; I'm too fat; it's hard to trust.

Maria distracted me from this train of thought by crawling between my legs and licking me. It felt good, but I couldn't let go. She was performing, waiting for me to perform. We weren't with each other.

I motioned for her to stop, to just hold me. She did. I began playing with myself and came in about thirty seconds. When I opened my eyes, I realized I had made another mistake. She was looking at me like I was a freak. I put my hand on her thigh, and she flinched.

"What are you doing?"

"Nothing," I said.

We lay like mollusks, each of us contained within her shell. She broke the silence with a surprising comment: "I like being gone down on but not tonight. I have my period."

"I'll do whatever you want," I said. It didn't make any difference to me how I pleased a woman as long as she had a good time.

"It's okay. I've kind of lost the mood."

I didn't push it; I was sleepy. As my thoughts began to blur, I lifted my head to say one last thing to her before I slept.

"Maria, you don't have to be insecure about your body."

"Thank you," she said softly.

When I woke up, I found Maria sitting on the end of the bed, fully dressed.

"Did you sleep well?" she asked.

"Fine."

"I didn't sleep at all."

I rubbed my eyes and patted the pillow next to me, but she ignored my invitation. I spied a clock radio on a night table beside the bed and saw it was seven in the morning. On the wall above the bed was a framed poster I hadn't noticed earlier. It was a black and white photograph of an extremely muscular ass and back rising above a sheet. The head and face were invisible.

"Do you like it?" Maria asked.

I thought it was tacky but said, "The person has a great butt. Is it a guy or a girl?"

"What would I be doing with a picture of a man in my bedroom?" she demanded.

"I don't know. Maybe you like gender ambiguity?" I suggested hesitantly.

"Do I look like someone who's into gender ambiguity?" Maria bellowed.

I didn't answer: I didn't appreciate being yelled at.

She yelled some more. Stalked out of the bedroom.

I got up and dressed as quickly as I could. I followed her into the kitchen where my boots were and began to lace them up. I wondered if I should just leave. She was staring at me like I was a big nothing.

"You seem really mad at me," I said.

"No, I'm not," she insisted. "It's just we're obviously totally sexually incompatible. Sex with you was terrible. I never want to have sex with you again."

My mouth dropped open. I usually had something to say but not this time. I had reached the same conclusion as Maria, but I thought the problem had more to do with her attitude than what we did and didn't prefer in bed. The last time I'd felt this yucky about a sexual encounter had been when I was straight.

Maria insisted on driving me home, and I let her because I was too scantily clad for public transit. This time, I noticed she didn't open the door of her truck for me. She whipped across the expressway while I stared out the side window. When she exited onto Jameson, I broke my silence.

"Listen. Sex for me is not about coming. It's not about one particular act. It's about having fun and taking care of each other's needs."

Maria thought about this for a moment and then said, "You're probably right. I'm sorry."

"Do you want to have breakfast?" I didn't know why I was asking. She was a jerk, but I kept holding out for her to be sweet so that the crummy feeling inside of me would go away. It reminded me of when I was fifteen and got involved with an older guy who worked at my parents' store. I kept waiting for our relationship and the sex to get better. Maria took me back to that time when my insecurity, unhappiness, and clueless optimism were twisted together in a lumpy braid.

"I'll call you," Maria said.

I suspected it was the last thing she would do.

I made her let me out on Queen Street. I was fed up with her faux chivalry, and with all the sex workers in my 'hood, I didn't look out of place sweeping past the roti shops in my lingerie and army boots. Dana, Veronika, and I lived together in an old house south of Queen that

Veronika had bought for a low price in a power of sale. She couldn't afford to live in it on her own and asked us if we'd be her roommates.

Dana had shut me out after we split. She was hurt; I hadn't loved her the way she had loved me. She didn't want to see me, didn't know when she would be ready. I called her every month for eight months; she was short, bitchy, blank. On what I decided would be my last attempt at connecting, I left some zines in her mailbox. Zines by and about transsexual women. She left a message on my answering machine, thanking me and suggesting coffee. She rescheduled twice and showed up late. I swallowed my irritation along with my espresso and told her I loved her and missed her. She didn't say it back, but we talked for a long time.

Shortly after, Veronika suggested living together. Dana and I liked the idea, especially since we weren't keen on our respective roommates, though we balked when we saw the house she had bought. It was crammed with junk, and holes were punched into the walls. A red shag carpet not only covered the floors but also mysteriously extended up the walls of the bathroom. There was even a fuzzy crimson cover for the toilet lid. Veronika, with her experience as a property manager, drew our eyes to the high ceilings, the crown moldings, and the spaciousness of the rooms. She hired her cousins to paint and drywall, and rented a giant machine from Home Depot and sanded the floors, revealing old parquet with a reddish gold sheen like chestnuts in the sun. Over the course of a few months, she'd made the home as stylish as she was, and Dana and I moved in.

As I unlocked the door, Dana's cat, Kaspar, a large white Burmese, brushed past my bare legs. Bacon and coffee smells wafted from the end of the hall. I realized I was starving and went into the kitchen to cadge some food.

Diamond whistled at my getup. "Girlfriend!" she said. She could be a frat boy and a fag in the same moment.

Veronika, who was toasting waffles, turned to see why Diamond was making a fuss. "I guess you spent the night with Maria. I was having a cigarette and saw you get into her truck."

"Tell us what happened!" Diamond waggled her fingers at my face. "C'mon, I'm peer."

Veronika did spirit fingers. "I'm pressure."

Their prompting was unnecessary; I was dying to share. I was also dying to get out of my clothes. "Let me get changed."

As I pulled on shorts and a T-shirt, I thought that having sex should be more fun than describing it to Veronika, but sometimes talking to her about it was the best part.

I grabbed a plate of food and sat on one of the vinyl stools Dana had brought home from work. "The Windmills of Your Mind" was playing on the boom box we kept on top of the fridge. I loved that a mod fashion icon was a femme dyke. Veronika knew a gay guy who had lived in the same apartment building when Dusty lived there with Carole Pope, and we had pressed him for his scant memories of them.

Between bites of waffle, I described my evening. Diamond howled with laughter, even at the parts of my story I didn't think were funny. She wasn't the most sensitive woman. Veronika told her to shut up, which made her more hyper.

"My problem is ..." Diamond paused to angle her face away from an imaginary camera. "I'm too good in bed."

Veronika shoved her shoulder. "Too confident."

"You know it, baby."

I popped the last piece of bacon into my mouth. Though my diet was largely vegetarian, I always caved in the presence of bacon. "Veronika, do you remember Holly telling us Maria was too controlling? Do you think she meant in bed?"

Veronika frowned. "She didn't have any complaints in that department. You know Maria was Holly's first woman, right?"

"Really?" I had no idea Holly had been more inexperienced than me when we made out. "Are you sure about that?"

"Yeah, she was a fag hag when we first met her. You know Splenderella, the black drag queen who does bingo nights? I just found out she's the father of Holly's kid. Holly and Splenderella were together from when they were thirteen to twenty, even though he's more or less gay."

"Interesting," I said, though I was preoccupied by my ghastly time with Maria. "I've never had sex with a woman who was so rigid."

"Personally, the whole being thrown down and fucked with a dick sounds perfect to me," Veronika observed.

"I love it when you fuck me like that," Diamond chimed in, giving both of us an unembarrassed smile.

I looked away. Veronika was so lucky to have a hot butch who clearly had a more egalitarian approach to sex than that macho idiot Maria.

As I attended classes and worked at the diner and volunteered at a prison library, I thought about Maria. I hoped she wouldn't call because I was afraid I wasn't strong enough to tell her to fuck off. Afraid because I imagined her telling me she was sorry, that I had pulled out her feelings and vulnerabilities like soft taffy and it had scared her. In this scenario, we fucked again and took turns being on top.

I was so relieved that she didn't call.

On the Same Team

Toronto, 1994

In an inner-city gym that smelled like sweat, Dana found herself surrounded by lean, nimble women dribbling and shooting baskets in organized lines. She had joined Lavender Hoops, a lesbian basketball league, even though her experience playing team sports amounted to a few humiliating memories in junior high of being a too short, too skinny boy picked near the bottom for teams. Well, she wasn't a boy anymore and at 5'7" wasn't too short.

Dana had asked Veronika if there was somewhere to meet dykes besides clubs and was informed the alternative was sports teams. Basketball was less intimidating than hockey, since she knew how to play. When she was a kid, her father had put up a hoop for her and Dawn and taught them one-on-one. Now, standing on the sidelines of the court, she couldn't remember a single rule. On top of that, she was dressed wrong. From a wardrobe inspired by Siouxsie Sioux and Tank Girl, she had dug out a ripped Marilyn Manson T-shirt, jean shorts, black leggings, and Converse low tops. The women around her were wearing puffy sneakers and athletic shorts. She sat down on a bench, wondering whether she should go home, when a tall woman with crooked teeth tapped her on the shoulder.

"Hi, I don't think I've seen you before. I'm Barb Brooks." She stuck her hand out.

Dana clasped her hand. "I'm Dana. This is my first time."

"Don't worry, there's always a few beginners." Barb touched a strand of Dana's hair. "Next time, put your hair back. And you'll need to take out your earrings. You don't want to have someone accidentally tear one out."

Dana fingered the numerous silver hoops on her earlobes. How sweet of Barb to think of her safety! Maybe this wasn't such a dumb idea. She followed Barb to a group of women huddled in a corner of the gym.

The following week, Dana wound up on Barb Brooks' team. Everyone on the team called each other by their last names, as though they were schoolboys. There were no designated captains, because that was too undemocratic, but unofficially each team had a leader, a woman who, by virtue of her skill, would call the plays and decide on a lineup; on Dana's team, Brooks was that person. She had played varsity basketball. When cornered, she could charge through taller players and sink baskets from anywhere on the court. She was also encouraging to rookies.

On Dana's fourth night, someone fouled against her, and she got a free throw. She stood with the ball clutched to her stomach in a state of despair, while her team and the opposing team stood in lines across from each other. The ref blew the whistle, and she wildly threw the ball. It narrowly missed the referee's head.

"Nice try, Dempsey!" Brooks yelled.

Yeah, right. Dana knew she was the weak link on the

team, but neither Brooks nor anyone else held it against her. She doubted she would be treated as well on the opposing team, which was led by Cavaco, a handsome blonde butch with anger-management issues. Cavaco constantly challenged the refs and socially excluded the women on her team who weren't jocks. She liked to win, and her team often did. She usually played centre. She ran fast and was a good shot, but her real talent lay in elbowing everyone else out of the way and grabbing the ball. When Cavaco made a particularly aggressive play against a teammate, Dana made a catty remark about her to Brooks, who said, "Guess you don't think she's hot?"

Dana shrugged. She didn't feel like explaining that for the most part she liked femmes. At least Brooks was comfortably offhand with her being a dyke. She assumed Brooks knew she was trans. Hormones had softened her skin, and she now had breasts, but the gay world, more attuned to the size of someone's wrists and scarves artfully placed to hide an Adam's apple, was a hard place to pass. What Dana could never decide was whether that was good or bad.

"Everyone else thinks she's hot," Brooks continued.

"The problem is she knows it," Dana replied.

Cavaco was solidly built, and her muscles were flat and as hard as tin, a fact she flaunted in ribbed T-shirts and tight, faded jeans. Then there was her perfectly worn black leather jacket and the fact that she drove a motorbike. She was the kind of oh-so-cool butch Veronika and Liberty would swoon over. It was sort of depressing the way masculinity, something Dana wanted to eradicate from her being, was so embraced, so desirable in this community she was supposedly part of. She had thought that Liberty didn't want to be with her because her body could never be female enough, but it was more complicated than that. Dana not being a butch was also a problem.

Did every femme want a butch and every butch want a femme? It had seemed that way to her until the night she discovered some of her butch teammates wanted each other. She was in the locker room, a place she always dawdled, waiting to be alone to use the one shower that had a door. Being in a room full of naked women was supposed to be normal, but Dana felt as if she were trespassing in territory where she didn't belong. She still had a penis, and tucking was impossible when you were charging up and down a basketball court and constantly squatting and swivelling.

Tonight her attempt to shower last had been foiled by Brooks' chivalry. "Ladies first," Brooks had said without irony, which had been cool. Dana stepped into the shower with her clothes on, undressed, placed her sweaty gym clothes in a pile just outside the shower stall, and got dressed after in a toilet stall. Now she stood in front of the large bathroom mirror, applying her lipstick, while beside her in a towel Brooks was slicking her hair back with gel. Behind them, Cavaco lingered in the doorway, dressed and fidgeting, her motorcycle helmet tucked under her arm. She seemed to be waiting for Brooks, who was telling Dana a story.

"This woman at work asked me if I didn't wear makeup because I was a Christian. Can you believe it? I'm totally out, too. I guess no one told her."

Dana smiled. "People make interesting assumptions."

Cavaco growled at Brooks. "Would you hurry up?"

Brooks turned and gave her a cheeky grin. Then she began to ever so slowly put the cap on her bottle of gel.

Cavaco picked up a wet towel someone had left on the floor and flicked it at Brooks.

"You jerk." Brooks grabbed at the wet towel, and as she did, the towel covering her body slipped, revealing her small breasts. Dana tried not to stare at her lovely, fit form. Then she became aware of Cavaco openly studying Brooks. Dana grabbed her makeup bag and slunk over to her locker in the adjoining room.

Everyone else had left, either to go home or to the bar. Dana shoved her boots and coat on and was about to leave when she realized she'd left her lipstick behind. It was Guerlain, so she went back to retrieve it, and discovered Brooks and Cavaco getting it on!

Brooks was naked, pinned by one of Cavaco's sturdy muscular legs to the tiles of the wall while Cavaco was fully dressed. The two of them were kissing with the same fierceness they showed on the courts, dipping their whole heads into one other. Dana stared, wondering why they hadn't at least gone into a stall. When they noticed her watching, they immediately broke apart.

"Sorry, I lost my lipstick." Dana felt herself flush.

Shit, shit, shit. She'd probably get banned from the league now. They would say she was a man, a sleazy male pervert trying to get a peek. She scanned the sinks, observing Brooks' gel tipped on its side next to Cavaco's motorcycle helmet, but didn't see her Guerlain anywhere. She felt her hands shaking and dashed out of the room. When she got outside the gym, she lit a cigarette and walked as quickly as she could to the subway station.

She could have joined the other women at the pub around the corner. That would have been the sensible thing to do, be casual and not act as though she had committed a crime. A transgression! Ha, ha. But the times she had hung out with her teammates, she'd felt bored. It took a lot of beer before bar conversation shifted from banter about the game to anything else. Once, conversation had ventured into the personal realm, but in a way that had been worse. The women had talked about knowing they were dykes when they were little girls because they had lopped off their Barbie's hair or were only interested in her camper. Dana remembered being horribly envious of Dawn's Barbie, but the gals in Lavender Hoops seemed to think dyke equals butch. Hanging out with them felt like hanging out with her boss and his boyfriend. They were part of the same queer family but a different branch from her.

Sadly, her branch was hard to connect with. A lot of trans women in her support group had problems with substance abuse and were working as escorts. Their casual references to abusive boyfriends and protecting themselves with tire irons and pushing drugs up their ass to get through weekends in jail was just too crazy for her. Then there were the lesbian trans women who lived in the suburbs and had very straight backgrounds—wives they were in the process of divorcing (their wives couldn't conceive of being dykes), kids who were angry and embarrassed, and careers they were being kicked out of or wanted out of (often in macho fields like construction, trucking, and the military—overcompensating, they explained). Her tribe, to the extent that Dana had one, was Liberty and Veronika.

Before she even unlocked the front door, Dana could hear music blasting, which meant her roommates were home, probably getting ready to go out. Liberty viewed Veronika as a bit of a mean girl, saw herself as the nice, nerdy one, but Dana had always been struck by their similarities: They were funny, direct, and had one button—on. Before Dana could take her first sip of coffee in the morning, Veronika would be nattering on her cell phone about property values and making plans with friends while telling her mother, who called three times a day, that she was too busy for lunch. Meanwhile, Liberty would set down the book she was reading and ask Dana if she thought capitalism could work.

Who could say what would work? Who would have thought living with your ex and the person your ex had been hung up on when you were together would work?

In the living room, Veronika was leaping on the couch while lip-syncing to a Billy Idol song. She had transformed herself into him. Cut her hair and dyed it blonde, lined her eyes with black, and decked herself out in black leather pants, vest, and fingerless gloves. When she spotted Dana, she jumped off the couch and slid to her knees, lip-syncing "Eyes Without a Face." "Such a human waste your eyes without a face," she sang, her features contorted in faux agony.

Oh right, it was drag king karaoke night. Dana had conveniently blocked it from her mind. Veronika was organizing it, and an invitation had been extended to her, but she had lied and said she was going out with her teammates. "Bring them!" Veronika had suggested, and Dana had been non committal. She didn't have enough distance from living as male to enjoy the campiness of dressing up as one.

Veronika grabbed her bulging crotch. "What do you think?"

Dana thought she was trying too hard. "I wouldn't sit next to you on the subway."

Liberty shuffled in looking equally sleazy as a white rapper. Her hair was stuffed under a tuque, her breasts were bound beneath a green Celtics tank top, and her juicy bottom was hidden in baggy track pants. The Reeboks she wore to work were on her feet, and a gold chain so thick it was more like a trophy swung from her neck.

Veronika lurched over to Liberty and gripped the chain. Her rocker dude persona dissolved into hysterical drag queen as she shrieked, "Where did you get that insane bling?"

"Value Village. I was going to go as Beck, but I was afraid no one would get it." Liberty slipped a disc into their CD player and started jumping around to "Bust a Move." Watching her pump the air with her fists, Dana thought she might be able to pass. Liberty was taller, with a less feminine face than Veronika, which helped, but she was also good at imitating masculine gestures, the controlled way most men moved their bodies. She had, after all, worked in an all-male-but-Liberty environment for years.

Dana retreated to the kitchen, where she took a bottle of white wine out of the fridge and poured herself a glass. Liberty had arranged their fridge-magnet poetry into a Simone de Beauvoir quote: "One is not born but rather becomes a woman." Hadn't Dana become a woman, a dyke? If so, why did she still feel like she didn't fit in? The Lavender Hoops gals were nice enough, but no one was attracted to her. It was the same in the club scene where Veronika and Liberty hung out.

She took a gulp of wine and went back into the living room and parked her butt in front of the couch and stretched out her legs. Her calves felt tight. That was the problem with exercising only once a week. Her more energetic roommates were dancing to another song. When it ended, Veronika said they should get going.

"Are you sure you don't want to come with?" Liberty asked.

Dana shook her head.

Liberty observed her nearly empty wineglass. "Did something happen at the game?"

Ex-girlfriends knew you too well. Dana sighed. "I caught these women having sex in the bathroom, and I'm afraid they'll think of me as a pervy guy. I'm worried I'll get kicked off the team."

Liberty frowned. "They were the ones having sex in public."

"That doesn't matter." The rules were different for Dana. No matter how she acted, what she had done to her body, she was still a *transsexual* woman, a *transsexual* lesbian, and that qualifier meant being treated differently, or at least having to worry about it.

Veronika kneeled down, putting her hand on Dana's shoulder. "If anyone tries to throw you out of the league, I will organize the biggest protest ever, okay?"

Dana mutely nodded. Felt tears well up. Hormones, mood swings; she had to admit she hadn't been entirely prepared for them. Yet a part of her took pride in the swirl of her emotions; they made her more female. She turned back to Veronika, who was asking if the women having sex were hot.

"Definitely. They're both butch, though."

Veronika wrinkled her nose. "Seriously?"

"Uh-huh."

"I've heard about this new butch-on-butch thing, but I just can't see one butch saying to another, 'You're so beautiful.'"

"They'd say, 'You're so handsome,'" Liberty interjected. "You and the drag king whose pants you want to get into can tell each other that tonight."

"Speaking of, we really need to leave."

The girls-dressed-up-as-bois took off. Dana thought about Cavaco and Brooks. "You're in great shape, buddy" is what they would say to each other, assuming they said anything at all. She couldn't shake the image of the athletic but decidedly female bodies of her grappling teammates. It was kind of nice to be having sexual thoughts. Estrogen had dampened her drive, made erections almost impossible. And when she did get them, it felt weird touching a part of her body she wished didn't exist.

Dana's final month in the league sped by. She didn't think she'd play on the team again, but her skills had improved. She had a sole talent: She was good at passing the ball. While her ability to do so was fuelled by terror at having to shoot or dribble, she was able to focus, find a teammate who was in the right position or could get into one, and throw the ball to her.

In the final game, her team lost to Cavaco's team. Neither Cavaco nor Brooks got most of the baskets, which was un-usual. Cavaco didn't hog the ball for a change and let her teammates do the scoring. And Brooks, generally so composed, couldn't sink a thing. Fortunately, the rest of Dana's team was in perfect accord. They played tough D and didn't flub any passes. They all scored, Dana getting an unprecedented two baskets. Despite Brooks' poor showing, after the game ended, the team voted her Most Valuable Player.

When Dana walked into the locker room to change, she felt excited and wanted to celebrate. She had gotten through the season! She took a long shower, dried her hair, and put on some fishnet stockings and a red dress with her Doc Martens. She was about to join her team at the pub when Brooks stormed in.

When she spotted Dana, she tried to smile. "You were great tonight! Two baskets—wow!"

Good to hear, but that didn't explain why Brooks slumped down on a bench, looking miserable.

Dana sat down beside her. "Are you upset we lost? You shouldn't be. We had a great season, and you're MVP."

"That's just it. I let everyone down." Brooks put her head in her hands. "I broke up with Cavaco last weekend, and I felt so guilty about it I lost my killer instinct. Then, after the game, I found out she's already seeing someone on her team."

Dana put her arm around Brooks' shoulder. "That sucks. I mean, that you found out after the game."

Brooks smiled a little. "Yeah." She gave Dana a quick kiss on the cheek. "You're sweet."

Sweet, Dana thought. *I'd like to be more than sweet.*

After drinks with her team, Dana was propositioned. Not, alas, by the teammate who asked if she could touch her fishnet stockings. Dana had let her, feeling like an exotic animal being petted, which she supposed was how the girls saw her, but her teammate's touch was so gentle and tentative all she could think was, *Yes, honey, please touch me.*

Nope, the offer for sex came when she clambered out of the streetcar, and a guy looked her up and down and murmured, "How much, Legs?"

Dana stared at him. A black guy in his twenties with Jheri curls. Was she passing? *Does he think I have a pussy or a dick?*

"A hundred dollars? C'mon, Legs," he pattered.

She'd never had sex with a guy before. She didn't want men, but the fact that he saw her as a hot woman? That was appealing.

He upped his offer. "A hundred and twenty."

She put her hand on his cheek. It was so bristly! The most magical thing about transitioning was how soft and smooth her skin was. For months, she had stroked her hands and cheeks with delight. No, she definitely couldn't have sex with him.

"Sorry, I'm not for sale." This in a gentle tone, as though she regretted having to turn him down.

He looked surprised. Almost but not quite flattered—which was exactly how she felt.

Disrobing

Toronto, 1995

I met Lisa at my new job at a law firm library in the Financial District. Like Lisa, the job was something I didn't think could possibly suit me. I joked with my father that my position was "strictly fifth column," while secretly feeling proud at being taken on at such an elite place. The work was interesting, but the environment was a culture shock. Everything I was used to discussing with co-workers—drugs, sex, politics, and classic rock vs. hip hop—was either inappropriate or not of interest. Along with mastering the intricacies of legislation and DOS-based databases, I learned to stick to such riveting conversational gambits as "Did you have a nice weekend?"

I had to purchase a new wardrobe since I had no suitable clothes. I bought some black and grey cardigans, black turtlenecks, and slim trousers (white, black, tan) that I wore with black ballet-style flats. My aim was to emulate Audrey Hepburn, and sitting in an oak chair behind a reference desk with a marble-topped counter, I did feel as though I were in an old movie. To my left were heavy wooden bookshelves lined with statutes and reports of cases, and on a shelf to my right was an unabridged *Oxford English Dictionary*, complete with magnifying glass to read the impossibly tiny font. Much of my work was what librarians and lawyers had been doing for decades, while other tasks, such as trawling through expensive databases that charged by the minute, were as modern and unrelenting as the capital markets the firm served.

My crush on Lisa, a lawyer, was inconvenient since she was unavailable. This I discovered when I bumped into her at the gay film festival, holding hands with a woman who looked familiar. Did she also work at the firm? It was a large place, so I wasn't sure, but something about her made me think she was also a lawyer.

Inconvenience aside, *I* couldn't understand my attraction to Lisa since she wasn't my type. I didn't mean she was femme. No, I could see she was butch. There was the ease with which she inhabited her tailored suits and the awkward way she carried her purse, as though it were a bag of rocks. There had also been her description of almost losing said purse—"I just set that puppy down for a minute." But she was a butch who could pass for straight—a slender woman with blonde hair to her shoulders and attractively bland features that included a slightly upturned nose and eyes the colour of smoke. Were her good looks the reason I was crushed out on a Bay Street lawyer who ran marathons? I didn't want to think about her record collection or how she'd vote in an election.

These were excellent reasons for me NOT to want to grab her and kiss her when we were both in the elevator, me in my work clothes and she in a tracksuit, sweaty and dishevelled from a lunchtime run. But nothing curbed my desire, including her obliviousness to me. While she was often in the library, our conversations rarely strayed beyond work requests, such as "Can you get a nineteen seventy-seven regulation for me?" Sometimes when we didn't have a reason to talk, the silence between us had a charged feeling, as though we were waiting to be alone so we could have a real conversation.

One day we had a fight. The day began with rush requests: stock exchange data from Australia for a prospectus, a search through all the legal dictionaries for an obscure Latin phrase. As I was heaving half a dozen tomes to my desk, Lisa strode into the library. "Can you track down labour regulations affecting miners in Guinea?"

I looked up at her. The skin beneath her eyes had a smudgy quality as though she hadn't slept lately. "Assuming the country has such legislation, not easily."

She handed me a slip of paper with a number to charge the client and told me firmly, "I need this as soon as possible. I don't care if you have to call law firms in Africa."

By early afternoon, I tracked down what she was looking for and emailed her that the legislation she wanted was at the reference desk. At five o'clock, the twenty-five-page fax from an African law library was still sitting there. That pissed me off—I had really hustled to get that information for her. I scooped up the fax and headed down the internal staircase to her office. Her door was open and I barged in.

"I think you forgot something." I held out the fax.

She absently reached for it. "Thanks," she murmured while her gaze sunk back to her computer screen.

I remained where I was until she looked up and asked me if there was something I needed.

"If a request isn't a genuine rush, it isn't fair to the other lawyers to say it is because you jump the queue." My face reddened. "It isn't fair to me either. I worked through my lunch hour for you."

Now I had her attention. She got up and shut the door. Her eyes met mine evenly. "I do need that legislation. I'm distracted, that's all. I'm having problems at home."

This was not remotely a direction I had expected our conversation to go in. "I'm sorry."

"I'm sorry for inconveniencing you." Her cool tone told me I was dismissed.

I hesitated at her door. "If you want to talk, you know where to find me."

Over the next month, our interactions only took place through email. If she needed a book, she sent her assistant to get it. I wondered if she was avoiding me, if she regretted discussing her personal life. Then, late one afternoon, she turned up in the library and asked if I had plans for the evening. Her tone was polite, casual. The only reason I knew this was not an indifferent query was because she never bothered with small talk. There was also the way she had waited in the stacks until no one was around before approaching me. I told her I had no particular plans.

"Would you like to go out for a drink?"

It felt like there was a pinwheel spinning in my chest. "Yes."

She brought me to a restaurant where I imagine she dined with male clients; the place was all dark wood and black leather booths and had one item on the menu, steak and fries. "If you're a vegetarian, they can accommodate you,"

she said. Our drink had turned into dinner.

Over shockingly tender steaks, I asked what made her choose the work she did. Maybe she didn't want to be a lawyer? Her dad was a famous judge, and tales imparted to me by unhappy articling students whose choice of a law career had been dictated by their successful fathers made me feel fortunate for the first time that my own family had so utterly abdicated their role in preparing me for my future.

"During law school, I had a summer job at a boutique labour firm. I defended two clients; one had sexually harassed his female co-workers and the other constantly missed work because he was a drunk. That's when I decided it didn't matter which so-called side I was on."

I didn't quite follow, and she had to explain that in labour law, you could represent the unions or management.

"What about regular people who get fired?" I asked.

"They can't afford me."

"And you think it's fair to always represent the rich and privileged?" As I said it, I realized it wasn't just her—it was also me. Only big firms with big clients could afford librarians.

"That's an access to justice issue," she said. "And of course I think ordinary people should have access. In fact, I pay for it. My law society fees pay for Legal Aid, not the government. But to your other point, a big firm doesn't necessarily guarantee a favourable outcome from the courts. A client responded to my opinion letter this afternoon by emailing me, 'Great, I'm screwed.'"

I looked at her. She was so articulate and knew so many things I didn't. I felt like my brain was being stretched, and it was exciting.

She was smiling at me. "Would you prefer to have dinner with a social worker?"

"I'm not a social worker," I replied. I had wanted a socially progressive job, but getting a position at the Toronto Public Library proved impossible without connections or starting in the system as a teenage page. Maybe she had a point about unions.

Lisa speared some skinny fries and asked how I'd wound up at the firm.

"I think they wanted to save money by hiring someone without experience." Among the Bay Street firms, ours was known for its big deals and its cheapness. My law background consisted of a volunteer gig at a library in a men's jail that had no legal materials beyond a solitary edition of *Martin's Criminal Code*. I had culled religious tracts no one wanted to read and catalogued adventure novels, westerns, and Easy Reading Books. "This is my first paid job in a library. I used to be a short-order cook."

"That's quite a change."

"Not as much as you'd think. When you're on the line, you have to do a dozen things at once for stressed-out waiters who want everything five minutes ago. It's the same at the firm, just substitute lawyers for waiters."

This was supposed to amuse her. Instead, she remarked, "You must think I'm a bitch. I'm sorry about the other week."

"It's okay. I shouldn't have gone to your office." I realized now that I had complained because I liked her and wanted her to see me as more than the hired help. Usually, I never took it personally if a busy lawyer had a meltdown or a hierarchical attitude towards me. "Did you become a lawyer because your father's a judge?"

If she was surprised I knew about her father, she didn't show it. Instead, she said, "My mother's also a lawyer, and, yes, I wanted to please them. That's not the only reason I went into law, though. I like the discipline it imposes on me."

"Why do you need discipline?"

She looked startled. "You should be a lawyer; you ask the right questions."

I thought of her jogging, the odometer she used to measure her steps. Lisa wasn't trying to be all that she could be; she was trying not to be something. What was she trying not to be?

I waited for her to say more. Instead, she flagged the waiter and paid for our dinner. Since it had been her idea and she'd chosen an expensive place, I broke my rule of always paying for myself.

We walked back to the firm. In front of our office tower, a fleet of taxis was waiting to take home all the lawyers who were working late. Yesterday, a female partner had asked me to send her a list of top speech therapists; her kids were speaking patois learned from their Jamaican nanny. This was probably the only chance I'd get to talk privately with Lisa. I summoned my courage and asked her if she was flirting with me.

"I'm very attracted to you," she said.

The whirligig in my chest started revolving again. I leaned towards her, and we kissed. A guy whistled and yelled, "Hey, pretty ladies." The last time I'd been hassled for kissing a woman in public we'd been called "fucking dykes." That woman had a crew cut, had been unmistakably butch. "Pretty ladies" was safer, but equally offensive.

We stepped away from each other.

I asked, "What now?"

"If you give me your phone number, I'll be in touch." She lifted her chin at the dude who had given us the dubious compliment. "We'll have to be discreet."

Discretion. I supposed this was going to be an affair. I supposed she still had a girlfriend. I wanted to ask but was afraid her answer might get in the way of being able to have sex with her.

People always think lawyers and librarians are secretly wild and naughty. "Lawyers did lots of coke in the eighties" was something I'd heard. Well, they didn't seem to be doing blow in the nineties. The one transgression at my firm had been a secretary accidentally emailing porn to everybody. The office was giddy for days; laughter could be heard in cubicles, bathrooms, the mailroom, conference rooms. It was a real morale booster, although a few male lawyers bitched about the fact that she wasn't fired, arguing that if a man had sent the email, he would have been tossed to the curb. Personally, I thought the shame of having to face everyone after sending an email with the subject line "Man with Big Cock" was sufficient punishment.

The next day, I brought a book Lisa had requested to her office. Unfortunately, she wasn't around. Later that afternoon, she approached the reference desk, stammered something as she handed me a note, and scurried out of the library. The note said: *The lingering scent of your vanilla perfume when I sat down at my desk was tremendously distracting.*

I was thrilled with this dry little note. I sent a reply sealed in an interoffice mail envelope with a similar tone: *So terribly sorry—I was trying to be helpful. I had no idea you were that sensitive to smell.*

Her reply came within half an hour, and I read it a dozen times: *I believe you knew exactly what the effect would be. I don't think it would be difficult for me to establish* mens rea. *Perhaps you would like to be punished?*

She thought she could punish me? Please. This prompted a less bantering response as we paced through the underground pedestrian walkway for twenty minutes after my day ended and before she had to meet a client for dinner: I told her what I liked in bed and asked about her preferences. My experience with Maria had taught me that communicating about this beforehand was important. What turned Lisa on? "You do. I'm open to new things." I was unable to pin her down further; we didn't use the same language. I was a librarian who classified my desire; she was a litigator who dealt in things that could be overturned.

On Thursday evening, we met at a downtown hotel. Again, I let her pay. As soon as the door to our room was closed, we began making out. She slid the hem of my dress up with both of her hands. When she saw my black lace panties, she paused to take a closer look at them. "*This* is what I want," she said. She wasn't speaking to me but to herself in a kind of wonder, and I realized the power of what I had to offer, of what she wasn't getting at home.

As though she were reading my thoughts, she said, "I told my girlfriend I was attracted to someone at work and, uh, she wasn't very happy about it. In fact, she broke up with me."

"Does she work at the firm?" I asked.

Lisa hesitated. "She's on secondment." This meant she'd been leased to a client.

"I see." So was I a rebound fling? Was that why we were at a hotel instead of my place? Or did she think I didn't live in a nice enough place in a nice enough neighbourhood? She had been surprised to hear I lived in Parkdale.

She took off my dress and stroked my ass. Then she laid me out on the bed on my stomach and kissed me. Her mouth landed here, landed there, my buttocks, my thighs, my back, my shoulders. I let her. I wanted to keep feeling the soft imprint of those lips on yet another part of my body. She was excruciatingly tender, and it was harder than anything I had felt in a long time.

When she flipped me over, she looped her baby finger around the lacy panel of fabric covering my cunt and pushed aside the material to eat me. Sensation thrummed through my body, and I came effortlessly. When I had done so twice, she lay on her back, waiting for me to do her. I liked that she expected this of me.

I undid the buttons on her Oxford cloth shirt and discovered she was wearing a padded bra. Her body was more petite and delicate than I had expected. I commented on this, and she stood on her knees and made me feel her calf muscles, which were like iron. She was boyish and ladylike at the same time.

She wanted me to taste her. She was pink and tidy and symmetrical, and when I put my mouth to her, I discovered less was more, that one finger and the barest pressure was all she needed to come. After she orgasmed, she burst into tears.

I knew some women did this, but I had never witnessed the phenomenon. I reached for her, and she immediately stopped crying. "I do that when it's intense," she told me. "I haven't had sex in a while."

"Why not?" I hadn't had sex lately either. I hadn't met anyone I was attracted to the way I was attracted to her.

"I didn't want my girlfriend."

"Why didn't you leave her?"

Lisa looked pained. "I was afraid of hurting her." She began weeping again. "I just lied. I had sex with my girlfriend last week. It was the first time in six months and it sucked. She was so fake I may as well have been paying a prostitute."

I didn't know what to say, wasn't sure how to navigate the transformation from crisp in-control lawyer lady to this emotionally raw woman. I kept my shoulder against hers as we lay together on our backs, our sweaty skin pressed into cool cotton sheets. When she rolled over on her side and began stroking my face, I asked her what she wanted.

"Sexually?"

I had meant, "What did she want from me?" But she obviously wasn't ready to answer that question. "Yeah, sexually. Tell me what you fantasize about."

She looked uncomfortable. "I have fantasies about men. Do you think that's weird?"

"No." What she was describing was common. Cock equals power, and power was a turn-on for many.

She was blushing. "I've never told anyone that."

"I'm shocked." I rolled onto my side and ran my hand over the hill of her hips.

She stretched her arms over her head. "I've never had sex with men, so I think that's why I fantasize about them. I just think about being fucked. I never think about men going down on me, just women."

The defensiveness in her voice was impossible to ignore, and the vulnerability in that turned me on. I stroked her breasts. "You misunderstand. I'm shocked you've never told anyone!"

Beneath my fingers, her nipples hardened. Perhaps to restore the balance of power, she asked, a bit sharply, if I fantasized about men.

"Truthfully, no," I told her.

"But you've slept with them?"

"Uh-huh." Oddly, the last person I'd slept with had been a guy. I'd had a fling with one of the cooks at my goodbye party after setting a few ground rules. "It works if they just do me, and for some guys, this isn't a problem. I guess you wouldn't know, being a gold star lesbian and all."

I hadn't slept with any other gold star lesbians. The butches I knew rarely had extensive histories with men but had managed to lose their virginity. Some experiences I'd heard about were deliciously weird. My favourite story came from Veronika's ex, Diamond, who had a threesome with two male models while on a Caribbean vacation. She had thought they were gay and in the closet and tried to bring them together by giving them simultaneous hand jobs.

The night after I slept with Lisa, she dropped by the library, holding two books. "I had to see you," she murmured in a low voice.

I took the books out of her hands and arranged to have lunch with her. It was raining outside, so we were stuck in a food court, eating sushi with yams and avocadoes and sharing a side order of edamame beans.

"I want to be with you," she told me. "Last night was perfect, but I'm afraid of fucking it up."

I scraped some wasabi sauce onto a sushi roll and then

covered it with a pink strip of ginger. Bit into sweet, salty rice. "I'm not sure what you're trying to say."

"I don't know," she replied unhappily. "I feel like I'm never good enough. Not at work, not at relationships."

I couldn't figure out what was going on. Did Lisa want to go out with me? It sounded as though she wasn't ready, but I wasn't ready to give her up. I pushed my food away and asked if she wanted to continue seeing me.

"Yes." She picked up my hand and kissed the centre of my palm.

I felt my underwear flood. If we continued to be involved, I'd have to keep some spare panties in my desk drawer. Our attraction was as intense and speedy as a time-lapse video, and I had no idea what we were going to do about it.

We kept getting together in hotels while she and her ex put their condo on the market. Lisa didn't spend the night with me, as she was trying to spare her ex-girlfriend's feelings. When her ex went out of town for business, we finally had a night to ourselves. We had sex for hours, fell asleep at midnight, and at five in the morning were feverishly fucking again, using our hands because we didn't want to interrupt our fun by brushing our teeth.

"God," Lisa sighed as she collapsed onto her back. "I can't remember the last time I woke up and had sex."

I didn't tell her this experience was a first for me. It was sort of stupid, but depending on whether or not you counted Dana when she was David, I'd never had a girlfriend, just flings and affairs. What we were doing felt like an affair but also felt bigger than that.

Lisa stared into my eyes. "You're so feminine. I love it."

"Thanks." I looked back at her. "I love being with you." What I didn't tell her was that I was pretty sure I'd fallen in love for the first time in my life. Last week, I had bumped into her on my lunch hour—she was in her running clothes, holding a cloudy green drink, and I felt so ridiculously happy to have unexpectedly come upon her.

She tucked herself into my side and pulled my arm over her. I'd never spooned a woman before. Most of the women I'd slept with were bigger than me, either taller or heavier, and I felt a little self-conscious around Lisa, as though I were an ungainly giant. In heels, I towered over her, though in bed I'd come to appreciate our height difference. Spooning her made me feel as tender and protective and possessive as a mama bear, along with things that weren't maternal, arousing thoughts and feelings that had to do with sex and power: *smaller creature that is mine to do what I like with.*

I kissed her shoulder. "You're my prettiest butch."

She rolled onto her back while remaining in my arms. "Do you think of me as butch?"

"Uh-huh."

"People never think of me as butch, but you're right; I'm not femme."

"I think butches are hot."

"Really? That surprises me."

"The whole butch/femme thing is about energy." Now I sounded like a fucking hippie.

"I'm the kind of dyke you can bring home to your

mother."

It had never occurred to me to choose my sexual partners on the basis of whether my parents would approve of
them. "My parents would be horrified by you."

She wriggled out of my grasp. "You're kidding! Why?"

"When I came out to them, they said they didn't care
if I brought home a woman or a man as long the person
didn't vote Progressive Conservative."

"I don't vote PC," Lisa said scornfully.

She didn't add anything. I knew she wasn't ready to
define whether or not we were having a relationship. This
was also why I hadn't pushed her to come to my place.
That and the fact that I was enjoying the adventure of
hotels I couldn't begin to afford. I got a kick out of the
desk clerks who were taken aback when Lisa signed out
four hours after signing in. More than one asked her, "Was
the room not satisfactory?" "No, it was perfect," she would
assure them. If I was with her (and I usually was), they
sometimes (but not always) realized we were using it as a
place to fuck.

I teased Lisa about her heterosexual fantasies. I threat-
ened to show up at the hotel with a man for her to fuck.

"You wouldn't," she gasped.

I shrugged. If we wanted a threesome, there were op-
tions; I was currently fielding a crush from a male articling
student. In the midst of my explaining the UK legal system,
he'd interrupted to ask if he could touch my shirt. I was
wearing a red silk blouse, and he was looking at it with a
dazed expression. In my most cool and matter-of-fact tone,
I'd replied, "No, because that would mean touching me,
which would be inappropriate," and continued describing

the categories into which the English law reports were divided. I hadn't minded his attentions, which were way less crude than I was used to in work situations.

Lisa was poking me. "Seriously, would you have a threesome with a guy?"

I shook my head. "No, because we'd have to hang out with him. That wouldn't *quite* be worth seeing you spread your legs for some cock." This, as usual, made her flush, which was what really got me off—embarrassing her.

She grabbed me by my shoulders and pushed me back onto the bed. Her blonde hair fell over my face like a soft sweet-smelling net. "Stop."

Of course *that* didn't stop me. "We could hire an escort. He could provide stud service, fuck you until you came, and then we could send him on his way."

Again, the idea of really doing this was horrifying, so I was rather surprised when she summoned me to her office the next day, closed the door, and suggested we go to Blue Steel, a male strip club in Mississauga.

I raised an eyebrow. "A strip club?"

She put her hand on my back, causing sensation to skim through me. "I'd like to know if I could respond to a man." This seemed to be a quest of some kind for her. "I doubt you'll find the answer at Blue Steel!"

"Yeah," she agreed. "I'll probably just want to make out with you."

The sheer oddity of her suggestion was intriguing. "Why do we have to go to the suburbs?"

"I don't want to see male strippers in the gay ghetto. I might run into some of the gay male lawyers I know."

We were back to discretion—naughtiness and discretion.

To get into Blue Steel, you had to enter the side door of a club where women stripped for men. Part of me wanted to abandon our project and just watch the women, but I followed Lisa down a set of stairs to a windowless basement room. There was no bar, just a stage surrounded by tables, chairs, and couches. While we checked our coats, a woman argued with the manager that her group had the VIP area. This turned out to be a circular black leather couch close to the stage, and her group was duly led to it. Whether this was desirable was an open question—I noticed a white stain I was pretty sure wasn't dried milk on the arm of the couch.

Lisa and I sat down on a pair of unsullied wooden bar stools and ordered drinks from the one waiter serving everyone. While I sipped a cosmo, I looked around. Most people seemed to be regulars—shirtless male dancers greeted table after table of women by their first names. Blue Steel was a community, and the crappy sound system, unfashionable setting, and diversity of the patrons was strangely reminiscent of a dyke bar.

An invisible MC announced our first dancer, Ace. Nirvana came on, and a super fit guy strutted onto the stage. He looked like an actor, the kind on a soap opera, with artful stubble and hair in a ponytail. He was also athletic. From an elevated ledge, he hurled himself into an impressive backwards somersault.

"He should be in a theatre program," Lisa shouted into my ear.

"Maybe he is," I replied. But I didn't think this was the

case.

When the song ended, Ace came over to our table and introduced himself. Even though I didn't think Ace was his real name, I told him mine.

Lisa remarked, "I see you're wearing Harley-Davidson boots. Do you have a bike?"

He looked surprised—his feet probably weren't what women usually looked at. "I used to. How about you?"

"No, but I like the idea of people thinking I do," she said.

He and I laughed. I liked the way Lisa could make fun of herself. All the cool, hot butches Veronika dated? I couldn't imagine any of them responding to Ace with that sort of quick self-deprecation.

Lisa asked Ace how hard it was to learn to ride, and as they chatted away, I got the feeling he genuinely liked her. Usually, it was I, not my lovers, who got the friendly attendion from men.. Even though Lisa was by conventional standards more attractive than me, in our relationship, I was the beauty and she the admiring one. Was that why the men around me were dancing for women? Did they want to be the pretty one, to have women in thrall to their bodies?

A black man appeared on stage. He was carrying a briefcase and wearing a suit and tie. The blazer and shirt soon came off. His chest was a classic Y shape, and his muscles were so huge they seemed to burst from his skin. He unbuckled his belt and whipped it against a bench. A woman rushed onto the stage and dropped to her knees in front of him with her ass in the air. Mr. Executive pretended to fuck her doggy style while gripping her hair in his fist. When they finally stopped, he pulled down his pants, displaying an erection in his briefs.

After leaving the stage, Mr. Executive made a beeline for our table. I supposed Lisa and I, having never been there before, were fresh meat. Mr. Executive told me his name was Michael, and I wondered if it was his real name since it was so unremarkable. He was older than I expected, close to forty, and pushy. I wanted him to go away, but he remained where he was, just behind me.

I pretended to be interested in what was happening on the stage. Then something interesting did happen: A dancer whipped out his dick and dangled it over the head of a woman sitting in the audience. All around me, women erupted, wild hyenas with prey in their midst—ARRRH!

Michael murmured in my ear, "You should try it sometime."

I turned around. "What, dancing on stage?"

"No, a penis on your head."

"I don't think so!" I said as though he had dumped a dead bird on my lap.

Michael stared hard at me for a few seconds before taking off. Even for someone as unsubtle as him, my repulsion had been impossible to ignore.

Lisa asked me what he had said, and I repeated our exchange. It felt as if he'd been hitting on me, the way a guy would in an ordinary bar. He wasn't trying to get my money; he was trying to get my attention.

"No private dance for him!" Lisa gestured to the corner where an L-shaped black curtain created a separate space.

I stared at her. "Are you planning on getting a private dance?"

"I'd rather go to my car and make out with you, but I

did come here ..."

We continued watching. I clapped politely for less-than-stellar performances. One young man, who was dressed as a construction worker, was especially awkward. The MC told us it was his first time, and I believed it. He was a pale kid who, unlike the others, didn't spend tons of time at a gym. He had no hair on his chest, and the hair on his head was sandy.

"He reminds me of Richie Cunningham from *Happy Days*," Lisa said.

I laughingly agreed.

"I'm going to hire him."

"Are you kidding me?" I asked. "What's wrong with Ace?" Before leaving our table, Ace had put his hand on the small of each of our backs. I had liked the soft query of his touch; it was the way I approached women.

"This kid doesn't have a clue. I think my experience with him will be more unscripted."

Lisa went over to the private dance area, which now had a lineup. A lot of overweight white women were getting dances from black men with hot bodies. Who, I wondered, had the power in that situation? No one ever talked about the privileges that came with looks, yet I was always struck by the extent to which people in social settings sorted themselves into groups by degrees of attractiveness.

When Lisa returned, she wanted to leave. I pointed to the stage. A group number from *Grease* had begun, and I suggested we go after the song. At the next table, a cute black woman was loudly admiring a black man on stage. "I could get up on that," she said, fanning herself with her hand. Her response to him was rather sweet, a loosening of sex roles. Not a reversal, though, for she, like all of us, was dressed up; men at strip clubs probably didn't shower and shave and put on their nicest clothes before heading out.

Outside in the car, Lisa put on a mix CD of sad, quirky girls (Björk, Tori Amos, Cowboy Junkies; her taste in music was less mainstream than I had expected) and drove back into the city along Lake Shore Boulevard. Looking out the window, I had a rare moment of missing Nova Scotia; I wanted to feel fog, smell the ocean, and see fewer people. She turned off the highway and parked the car in a lot overlooking the lake. I waited for her to tell me what had happened.

She sighed. "I tried to connect? But I forgot how inarticulate young men are. Any Mrs. Robinson fantasies I've ever had are gone."

I waved my hands in her face. "Start at the beginning."

"I sat on this bench with the kid hovering over me. I told him he was cute and asked him what kind of women he liked. It occurred to me he might be gay or bisexual, so I added, 'Or maybe you like guys.' He looked totally uncomfortable with that suggestion and said, 'No, just girls.' His homophobia was a little off-putting, but I tried to flirt with him anyway. 'Any special kind of girls?' I asked, and he gruffly responded, 'All girls.'"

My eyebrow flipped up. "What did you expect?"

She considered. "I guess if I'd been dancing, I would have come up with something friendlier, like 'I'm not very discriminating,' or 'Women who know what they want.' Anyway, the song began, and he told me I could touch him. He said this as though he were employed at Burger

King—you know, 'You can also get fries with this.' Since I couldn't imagine ever being in this situation again, I played with his nipple, which I don't think he was expecting. I felt absolutely nothing; I just thought, male nipples are so tiny, like the head of a pin. Around us on other benches, couples were humping, but I kept my body away from him, so he just ground his pelvis into the bench. I think we were equally grateful when the song ended."

"Oh, dear." I made a sympathetic face. "I hope you remembered to tip him."

"I did." She shook her head at herself. "I can't believe I suggested this. Thank God I didn't see anyone who looked like a lawyer."

I teased, "Maybe that kid's an articling student somewhere."

"Ha! He'd be at work right now."

I thought about how Blue Steel wasn't so different from work. At the strip club, people pretended to be naughtier than they were, whereas at the firm, people pretended to be nicer, but there was the same unspoken hierarchy and politeness. A politeness that came from a mix of kindness and fear, the kindness being a desire not to make people feel bad, and the fear being an unwillingness to unmask power, to challenge who has it and why.

"Lisa, why did we really go to Blue Steel?"

She looked at her lap. "Well, I do sometimes fantasize about men, but you're right; it is more complicated. I guess I don't always want to be who I am, you know—boring lawyer."

"Oh my God, you are the opposite of boring!" I squeezed her hand.

Lisa's eyes met mine uncertainly. "Also, I don't want to be bored with you. I have a tendency to get bored in my relationships."

I dropped her hand. "I'll try not to be boring."

"Liberty, please don't be mad. I like you so much. And I love the way we're so different. It makes it interesting."

It was true we were different. I'd never hung out with upper-middle-class kids, which made her downright exotic. What I knew about private schools was what I'd read in books. And my hippie family, the working-class neighbourhoods I'd always lived in, and my cooking jobs were probably hard for her to imagine.

I wanted to show her my world. "Can you stay over at my place tonight?"

She picked up my hand and kissed it. "Of course I can."

Happiness teemed through me. I told her my housemates were dying to meet her and hear about our night.

She let go of my hand. "What? I thought you said they were gay."

"They are." Except her gay and my queer weren't the same thing. I realized I hadn't gotten around to telling her Dana used to be my boyfriend David.

Unpacking the U-Haul

Toronto, 1997

The receptionist called the reference desk to tell me I had a visitor. I assumed a vendor was dropping off training materials since the articling students were starting next week. I'd just been reading their profiles. There was a former National Ballet dancer who had interned at the UN, and a rugby captain who played the trombone and spoke five languages. Lisa was similarly accomplished: varsity soccer, graduate degree from the London School of Economics, dean's list at the University of Toronto. Her ex (who had left the firm) had been the law school silver medalist. I worried about whether Lisa thought I was good enough for her.

Two months ago, Lisa had dumped me in the food court. I had told her Veronika was planning to sell the house, and I didn't know whether I should be looking for a place by myself, with her, or if I should continue living with my roommates wherever they landed.

"I want to know what we're doing."

Lisa said, "I don't want to live with you."

That was hard to hear. "Okay. Where do you see us going?" We'd been having our non-relationship relationship for almost two years. "Are we just about sex?"

Recently I had been thinking about Lisa's ex. The way

Lisa ended things—not making any effort to sort out their problems, lining me up to avoid being alone because Lisa hated being alone—was not so great. And while I knew Lisa and I were more sexually compatible than she had been with her ex, she had built a life with that woman and not with me. Then there was Lisa's straight best friend, another lawyer with whom Lisa trained for marathons and seemed a little smitten.

"This isn't just a sexual relationship." Lisa sounded totally annoyed.

"How reassuring."

"Fuck you."

I sighed. "That's helpful." Lisa either dodged problems or blew up. Then she'd apologize for getting mad while the conflict remained unresolved, a snarl hidden in my hair.

"You want to know what I want, Liberty? I want to break up." Lisa glanced at her watch. "And let's do it now because I need to get back to work."

Shock smashed through me. "You can't end it like this."

"Oh yes I can."

She stood up and walked away. I grabbed our trays and followed her. When she saw me step onto the escalator, she picked up her pace. I tore up the moving stairs as quickly as I could in a pencil skirt. I would have cornered her at the top had I not glanced up and seen my favourite research lawyer, who asked me if something was the matter. I realized I was still clutching the food trays. "Um," I said while Lisa jetted off.

At the end of the day, I'd called her to ask if we'd had a fight. No, it was over, she informed me. Relationships had natural endings, and it was best for us to move on before it got ugly. "I did love you," she said before hanging up the phone.

Walking home from work that day with the forlorn sound of Portishead pouring through my headphones had been the saddest trek of my life. I was so miserable I couldn't even talk about it with Dana and Veronika. I went to bed at eight and woke up at three, my mind pinging to the loss of Lisa. She wasn't in the office the next day or the day after that; her secretary told me she was in Bermuda.

Lisa had phoned me from her hotel on day four and told me she had changed her mind about breaking up. And I took her back because I was willing to do anything to have her back, to stop feeling so shitty.

Instead of a vendor with piles of training materials, I found Veronika waiting for me in the reception area.

"Do you and Lisa want to have lunch?" she asked.

"Lisa's running," I said. "She's preparing for another marathon. Also, she's got this big trial."

"That's too bad." Veronika got up from the plush leather chair. "I love her new haircut."

Recently, Lisa had begun to dress in a style she preferred—more masculine, more casual—telling me she didn't care anymore if people thought she "looked like a dyke." Her women's khakis and Oxford shirts had been junked for dark, stylish men's jeans and exquisitely thin cotton shirts purchased at upscale stores I'd never heard of until she led me into them. Yesterday at Coupe Bizzarre, Jimi had cut Lisa's hair so it was short and spiky and reminiscent of Laurie Anderson. Then he also brought Veronika back to the eighties with a sleek, layered Joan Jett cut.

Veronika stopped in front of a painting with an anticolonial theme painted by an up-and-coming aboriginal artist. Lowering her voice, she said, "That's edgy for a corporate law firm."

"What better way to appropriate the revolution than to buy it and put it on your wall?" I replied without bothering to lower my voice.

"Liberty! You're so cynical."

I punched the elevator button. "I don't mind that you aren't." Veronika's sincerity was one of her best qualities. For her, dancing *was* the revolution, but the club nights she organized were inclusive, raised money for charities.

We left my tower, and I led the way to a noodle joint. On the sidewalk, people whose professions I could pick out by their clothes streamed by: lawyers in sombre suits, investment bankers in flashier ones, secretaries in mall brands, IT guys in khakis, and messengers in shorts over long johns.

The noodle house was noisy. Young Asian women behind the counter yelled out orders to cooks, who tossed handfuls of ingredients into sizzling oil, and the end result was scraped out of aluminum woks with metal tongs. A waiter delivered our bowls of steaming egg noodles with peanut sauce and orange and green vegetables. I dug in.

Veronika didn't. "So, um, my mom's been diagnosed with pancreatic cancer."

I set down my chopsticks. "I'm so sorry."

She unclasped a boysenberry leather handbag to reveal a stack of medical pamphlets. "Her cancer is stage four. Is that a death sentence? I haven't read these yet."

"It's not good news," I replied cautiously.

"Oh." She shut her purse. "I thought it was bad, but

my mom didn't seem upset, which I guess should have told me something. You know what a Negative Nelly she is."

Though Veronika and her mother talked incessantly, the directness I was accustomed to in my family was not how they operated. Veronika had never had an actual conversation with her mother about being gay. Instead, she introduced Erzsébet to her butch lovers without ever defining the nature of the relationship. Perhaps her mother was equally oblique.

"Do you think your mom already knew about the cancer and didn't tell you?"

"She's been losing weight for a while, but whenever I brought it up, she had excuses." Veronika picked up a chopstick and pushed it into the fleshy part of her thumb. A few months ago, she had quit smoking. "I can't believe this. She makes everything into a drama, and when a real crisis happens, she keeps her mouth shut?"

"Do you want me to do some research about pancreatic cancer? Survival rate, alternative therapies, that sort of thing?"

"Sure."

Back at the office, I started flipping through the blue Dialog pages to see if we subscribed to any databases dealing with health information. My boss reminded me we had to attend a team-building exercise with the records and conflicts department.

The library staff took the elevator to a boardroom that had been cleared of furniture. A giant mat made up of squares had been thrown over the carpet. Three women from human resources split everyone into teams and told us we couldn't communicate except by hand signals. Each of us took turns walking on the squares, attempting to cross the mat. If we landed on a bad square, a human resources kicked us off. We had to remember which squares were bad and convey this information to our teammates without speaking, which meant a lot of furrowed brows and vigorous pointing.

The exercise struck me as absurd and dull, but I muddled along, not wanting to let down my teammates who got into the spirit of it. They were upset at the end when we lost and it was revealed that a few squares that started out as "safe" became "unsafe" as the game unfolded. The exercise was supposed to help us cope with change; the office was about to be renovated. I supposed that a game in which the rules changed and weren't communicated to us was an accurate metaphor for how little power we had.

Back at the reference desk, I had an email from Lisa inviting me to drop by. Her office door was closed, but her secretary gestured for me to go in.

When Lisa saw me, she looked pleased. If I had been wearing a mood ring, it would have shifted from yellow to blue. There were so many moods in our relationship, but it felt as though I were the piece of glass reflecting the changing temperature of her skin.

She rolled her Aeron chair over to me, picked up my hand. "My case just settled. I can come over tonight if you like."

"That would be nice."

"What's the matter? Are you mad at me?"

I shook my head. "I just had lunch with Veronika. Her mom has pancreatic cancer, stage four."

"That's terrible." She frowned. "Is there something we can do for her?"

"I hope so. I don't know."

On my way home from work, I stopped off at the health food store to pick up my favourite fennel-flavoured toothpaste. It was exciting that Parkdale now had a health food store. As I was leaving it, a guy asked me for change. Panhandlers were another new addition to the neighbourhood. Broke people didn't waste their time asking other broke people for money, so maybe Veronika was right that the neighbourhood was gentrifying and she'd get serious coin for the house.

I handed the guy five bucks. I wasn't usually so generous. Most people didn't bother to give. I didn't judge because it wasn't like I did it every day, even though the need was always there, and I could spare a buck on a daily basis.

The guy looked at the bill with happy astonishment. I wished it were as easy to please my girlfriend. When had Lisa stopped blushing in bed? The enchantment of us had evaporated, couldn't dispel the part of her that was never still, never satisfied, no matter how much she ran or threw herself into her work. You would think that growing up being told you were pretty and smart and special would make someone feel good about herself. But it didn't seem to work that way for Lisa, who was big on self-improvement—special diets, personal trainers, athletic challenges.

The silly change exercise from work made me wonder: Was Lisa one of those squares that had become unsafe, or had she always been unsafe?

Lisa called to tell me she would be late. Unexpected conference call plus a workout plus stopping by her apartment to collect her stuff and eat whatever she was allowed to eat on her current cleanse. I lay on the living room couch with a novel, waiting for her, unable to concentrate. Veronika was upstairs getting ready to go to the new lesbian bathhouse. She had disinterestedly eyed the information I had printed on pancreatic cancer and told me about her evening plans. My eyebrow shot up. It did that without my realizing it, easily telegraphing *you're-kidding-right?*

Veronika viciously mimicked my raised eyebrow.

I asked, "Is casual sex what you want right now?"

"As opposed to?"

A hug? I couldn't hug her, though. We didn't do that for some reason. It was strange because we both hugged Dana.

I sighed. "I don't know. Something emotional?"

"Liberty, you're so judgmental. It kind of pissed me off last week when you said my primary dating criteria is hotness. What do you think I should be doing? Sleeping with women who don't make me wet? What would that prove? Besides, it isn't as though Lisa is a woofer."

I put up my hands in surrender. Every one of her words was a spike on a wheel meant to prod me into a fight. She was blinking as though she were about to cry, which I'd never seen Veronika do. She was a mess and didn't realize it. She had recently been dumped and kept saying, "I'm the dumper, not the dumpee." To me, it sounded as though her ego rather than her heart had been crushed.

"Vee, I don't want to fight, okay?"

"Okay." She left me to my book.

The doorbell rang, and I ran downstairs to let in Lisa. I warned her Veronika was in a foul mood. A warning then contradicted by Veronika, who, when we passed her room, pranced out to show us her outfit. Her need for admiration was too naked, and I couldn't bring myself to provide any.

Lisa was more obliging. "You definitely know how to rock a kilt, though I've never understood the schoolgirl fetish. I always think of the brutish girls I played field hockey with."

Veronika pretended to thwack Lisa's feet with an imaginary hockey stick. "I'm putting on a different skirt."

We went into my room. I lay on my bed while Lisa did stretches on the floor.

She asked, "Do you know why Veronika and Claude broke up?"

I told her all I knew was that Claude had a new lover.

Lisa said, "Veronika wants the seamless butch, who doesn't exist. Butches aren't cool, emotionally shutdown men. They need to be able to cry in front of their girlfriend."

I didn't think Claude needed to cry; she and Veronika were both cool types who made other girls cry. Lisa, on the other hand, was a crier. She cried at movies, weddings, after a tense call with her mom, if she had PMS. Not that this meant she was in touch with her feelings—she just had a lot of them. It sounded as though she were describing *her* fears about dating a girl like Veronika.

I knew Lisa found Veronika sexy. She had been surprised to learn Veronika and I once slept together.

"You two? You're both femme." She paused. "What did you guys do?"

"God, you're sexist! I fucked her if you really want to know."

I was so busy being offended that only later did the implications of her words sink in. I'd teased her about it: "You've never asked me what I've done with a butch. I guess the idea of me and Veronika together turns you on, which makes you *so* different from the average straight guy!" She had blushed, and I had been amused.

Now jealousy curled around me like smoke. I stood up. "I'm taking a shower."

When I came back into the bedroom, Lisa surprised me by tugging away my towel, pulling me to her. Without entirely wanting to, I responded. People always said sex wasn't everything, and I'd thought that was naïve; relationships were always collapsing because the people in them weren't having sex. Lisa and I had been astonished at how good it was between us, so why did everything feel fucked up?

Lisa began kissing me, touching me. I didn't stop her, but I was silent, passive. When her hand hesitantly cupped my mound, my body gave me away—I was so wet her fingers slid into me. She sucked my moistness from her fingers, looking pleased.

I wanted to wipe the satisfaction from her face. I yanked her fingers from her mouth. "Time for you to put that tongue of yours to work."

She immediately obeyed. The Catholic girl in Lisa loved it when I talked dirty, loved garters and stockings and anything slutty.

As my climax built, I dug my fingers into the spiky strands of her hair and pulled. "You're so good at this. You're such a whore. A filthy little whore." There was a new edge to my words.

Lisa noticed. Before my orgasm had subsided, she looked up from between my legs. "You're mad at me."

"You're into Veronika."

She didn't deny it. "I'm still attracted to you."

I burst into tears. "I wanted more from you."

Wanted. Love in the past tense.

Different for Dykes

Toronto, 1997

When Veronika arrived at the bathhouse, dykes were hanging out on the sidewalk, locked out. A hot tub had broken down, and no one was sure how long it would take for the women to be let back in. One woman was trying to ramp up the sexual energy by reading erotic poems out loud. Would fags read each other poetry in this situation? Veronika doubted it.

Fuck erotic poetry. Fuck Liberty telling her she needed something emotional. Like it was so easy to separate your sexual needs from your emotional ones. Like everything in her life wasn't fucked right now—her mom getting sick, Claude dumping her for accidentally giving her genital herpes, which was really unfair. Veronika had read the safe sex pamphlets lying around at the bars and couldn't remember anything in them about not going down on someone if you had a cold sore on your mouth.

Forget about her. Claude had certainly forgotten Veronika. Gone off her like she was rotten meat and acquired a new lover as soon as the sores healed. *Guess it's my turn to find someone new.* There was even a woman she had in mind, Suzanne, one of the bathhouse organizers.

Women were heading into the bathhouse. Veronika

paid the $15 cover, and was handed a locker key and a fluorescent bracelet that could be offered to someone in exchange for a kiss. Then she was herded into a room where a buxom blonde femme in a magenta slip gave everyone a terse lecture about the broken hot tub: "Women failed tonight. They failed to take on the shared responsibility for our environment. When the hot tub overflowed, no one told a volunteer. We have to give the owner every penny we make for the damages, so if you see a problem, make *sure* you tell a volunteer right away."

I want a spanking, not a scolding! Veronika sashayed upstairs to the lockers and agreed to share one with a young, perky femme. As they deposited their handbags, Veronika realized she felt nervous. It had been a while since she'd picked up a woman, and she wasn't sure she had ever done so while sober. The bathhouse didn't serve alcohol.

"Too bad I can't get a drink," Veronika remarked to her lockermate.

The baby dyke responded with an eager smile. "I have rum in my car."

Yeah!

They headed back outside, where they collected a third woman, who was also younger. Veronika was twenty-eight, and the women turned out to be nineteen and twenty-two.

Inside the car, they took turns squirting a water bottle filled with booze into their mouths. It was so cozy Veronika almost didn't want to leave. The nineteen-year-old earnestly explained she was bisexual and wanted a sexual experience with a woman. She was fed up with telling guys no and having them get mad at her and not even want to be her friend, so she had decided to go after what she really wanted.

The other young woman said, "I'm queer. You could call me bisexual, but that makes my life sound more interesting than it is. Coming tonight is a big deal for me."

Veronika asked, "Is there someone here you're interested in?"

The woman blushed. "Yes. How did you guess?"

That's why most of us are here.

On the way back, Veronika spotted Suzanne locking up her bike to a railing. She was a cycling advocate who was super fit. Damn, she was cute with her rosy cheeks and dark curly hair and muscular legs she didn't bother shaving.

"Hey," Veronika called out. "What's up?"

Suzanne said she was working a volunteer shift at the door and complained she was tired; she'd just come from work.

"So what are you looking for tonight?" Veronika asked her coyly.

"I'd like to go home and go to bed."

That didn't sound promising. Nor did the fact that she looked uncomfortable. She gave Veronika a weak smile and disappeared into the bathhouse.

Veronika took a deep breath. She'd been blown off. Well, she was a big girl. Time to check out other possibilities.

The bathhouse was on two floors, each consisting of a hall with rooms along the sides. Walking through the space, she noticed some attractive women but didn't feel like flirting. Dykes had towels knotted around their waists, and it was like being at the Y. Veronika hadn't taken off her clothes, not because she was shy or embarrassed but because she felt as though her nudity should be someone's reward. Bored and realizing she was the only woman dressed besides the volunteers, she joined a game of strip Twister in progress on the lower floor.

Women crowded around the plastic sheet, shrieking and giggling. A volunteer turned the spinner, calling out combinations in a loud, cheery voice: "Blue, left foot; green, right arm."

Not far from the game, a naked woman lay with her head buried between another woman's thighs. These were the only women Veronika saw having sex, and they registered about as much interest from everyone as Pet Rocks might have.

Before long, Veronika was down to a lacy bra and thong. Another spin, and a redhead in front of her moved into a position that would have allowed Veronika to rim her.

"You better hope you don't fart," a woman called out to the redhead, and everyone laughed.

"Yeah, especially since I had beans for supper," quipped Red.

Fart jokes didn't let up for another five minutes. Like the woman who had beans for dinner, Veronika's hands were now on the floor, and her ass was in the air on display for the boisterous crowd. She could not have felt less sexy, and an old memory slipped into her head: Girl Guide camp, one girl holding open the door while she was using the outhouse, and Sharon, her first love, protectively slamming it shut. *If I saw Sharon now, would I be attracted to her?*

As soon as she could, she escaped. The most popular place was the sauna, and Veronika sauntered in. As she soaked up the heat in her bra and panties, she listened to a group of women, who apparently played hockey together, discuss camping trips. Interrupting with a cruisy leer seemed ridiculous. When her lockermate came in to ask for the locker key, Veronika followed her out. As the nineteen-year-old retrieved a water bottle, Veronika asked where her friend had gone.

"She took off."

They hadn't been here *that* long. Had things gone badly with the woman she was interested in?

The girl didn't know. Veronika asked her if she'd met anyone.

She shook her head. "How about you?"

Veronika shook hers.

"How about the woman you were talking to downstairs?"

"She wasn't interested."

Her lockermate made a sympathetic moue.

"It's cool." It wasn't though. Usually women fell down before her fabulousness!

At that moment, Suzanne ambled by and gave her a big grin before helping a girl who had lost the key to her locker. Had Veronika made a mistake? Suzanne's earlier rejection had seemed clear-cut.

Down the hall, Veronika passed the make-out room, which was empty. There weren't many women here. But on the opening night, when apparently there had been a huge crowd, Veronika didn't know of any dyke who had hooked up with a stranger. Dykes didn't seem to operate the way gay men did. Dykes, maybe most women, mostly sucked at being sluts, and she didn't think it had to do with shame or guilt or lack of horniness. *We're too damn picky.*

Veronika sat down in the lounge, brooding in her underwear. Maybe she should go home. She had to get up early tomorrow. She was having breakfast with her mother and looking at antique stores, which they did almost every week. *Shit, we might not be doing that for much longer.* Her dad had died of cancer, and that hadn't been any picnic. Coming home from elementary school and hearing him cry because he was afraid and in so much pain, and her mom losing it and getting plastered on wine. God, she had kind of forgotten about that. There was too much in her head tonight.

Suzanne left her post at the door and came over. "Having a good time?"

"To be honest, not so much."

Suzanne laughed. "Sorry to hear that."

Was Suzanne interested? Time to find out. Veronika held out the fluorescent bracelet she had been given at the door. "Seeing as you invited me here, I think you should kiss me."

"I didn't invite you. I gave you information about the event."

Ouch. This was bad, awkward. Veronika was about to coolly apologize when hands grabbed her wrists. Suzanne slammed her against a wall. Shoved her leg between Veronika's thighs and stuck her tongue down her throat. For a whole thirty seconds. As abruptly as it began, it ended.

"Good night," Suzanne said.

Before Veronika had time to process, Suzanne had grabbed her bicycle helmet and walked out the door.

What the fuck? Did she feel sorry for me? Gross!

Veronika went to her locker, dug out her stuff, and got dressed. As she was putting on her shoes, her lockermate turned up. She, too, was leaving. Heading back to Oshawa without any lesbian experience.

Outside, Veronika hailed a taxi. She didn't think her evening could get any more tedious until she and the cab driver had a conversation she'd had so many times before with so many men.

Cab driver: Pretty girl like you going home alone?

Veronika: That's right. ALONE.

Cab driver: Do you have a boyfriend?

Veronika: I'm gay.

Cab driver (sputtering): You like girls? A beautiful girl like you? Have you ever tried a man?

Veronika: I prefer sex with women.

Cab driver: But, but, but, what do two women do?

Veronika: Give each other multiple orgasms by any means necessary.

Two blocks from her house, right on Queen Street, she had him stop the cab. She didn't tip him, and he hawked the word *bitch* at her. A neon bar sign blinked at her, Happy Times, one of Parkdale's dive bars. Part of her wanted to go in and have a beer and play video poker, but the chances of doing so unmolested were slim.

At home she took vodka out of the freezer and made herself a drink. She discovered Lisa standing by herself in the living room, staring out the window and drinking wine straight from the bottle. Okay, weird. Veronika walked over to her.

"Hey," Lisa slurred. "How was your night at the bath-house?"

Veronika wasn't sure she wanted to get into it. "Sucked."

"Mine sucked, too. Liberty and I broke up."

"Really?" There hadn't been any big dramas that she knew of. Or, wait, they'd had a big fight, but hadn't that been months ago?

Lisa placed the empty wine bottle on the top of the sideboard and promptly knocked it over. She was drunk. "We really broke up."

"Why?"

Lisa lurched forward and put a finger beneath Veronika's chin and kissed her softly on her surprised lips. "Because I think you're hot."

Veronika's body reacted. Reacted the way it should have at the bathhouse but hadn't. Of course, she had always liked Lisa. When Liberty first turned up with her, Veronika had been impressed and envious of the tales of their hotel-room rendezvous. It had sounded so sophisticated.

She leaned into the comfort of Lisa's body, and Lisa clutched her ass, and they started making out. Veronika stepped away to peel off her thong. Then she took Lisa's hand and pulled her fingers into her. *Switch off everything but my body.*

What Gets Said

Toronto, 1997–1998

When I arrived at my cubicle, a strange man was peering at my computer monitor. "Excuse me," I said.

He turned around and I saw he was a she, a tall butch dyke with dark hair in a brush cut. A chunky men's watch was falling from her slender wrist, and the outline of large breasts was visible under a long-sleeved shirt. Her face was square, her jawline pronounced, and a few old acne scars were scattered across her cheeks below her glasses. Behind the glasses, her eyes were the colour of dark wood, and she had impossibly long eyelashes. She was rather attractive.

Not that I wanted to go there.

She gestured in the direction of my screen. "We're checking the printer sharing on the network."

"Will this take long?"

"Hard to say." She seemed to think this was funny.

I didn't bother hiding my annoyance. "Do you think you could get me a laptop in the meantime?"

"I'm already finished. I was kidding."

"Oh." Since I'd broken up with Lisa, I'd been in a state of huffiness. I reached for friendly. "Sorry for being impatient. I'm Liberty, the librarian."

"Beth," she replied. "I'm doing a contract in IS." Information systems.

"Good to meet you."

She nodded and left.

Seeing Lisa at work had been intolerable, especially after Veronika told me they were dating, so I'd found a job as a librarian at a major daily. Unfortunately I didn't have enough to do. The journalists preferred running their own searches, and the paper was losing money and cutting back on positions. I'd had a busy month with the recent death of Princess Di, going through the photo archive and clipping files for all things Royal, but mostly I indexed stories and ensured the online version of the paper was identical to the print.

I picked up a corrigendum that needed to be added to the online database. In a story about a police dog killed in the line of duty, the dog's name was printed as Biscuit when it should have been Brisket. Reading a quote from the cop in charge of the canine unit—"I keep stopping at the curb to wait for her. I can't believe she's gone, that she's not by my side"—I felt a spurt of grief, which surprised me. In disaster movies, the dog always survives, but I detested that false sentimentality about so-called innocents, animals and children. Whenever I saw cars with bumper stickers that said, "Baby on Board," I felt like putting a sign on my back that said, "Single and childless—kill me now." So why was I so sad?

I was sad for the same boring reason I'd been sad for the last ten months—Lisa. Angry, hurt thoughts of her twitched through my brain like dismembered limbs. I wanted to forgive her, but all she had offered me was a feeble lawyerly sorry-I-hurt-you apology, as though I had been overly sensitive. I wanted us to process, and she had said no, we could only hang out if we didn't discuss what had happened, if we just "moved on."

I hadn't been (entirely) celibate, but I hadn't moved on. I needed to fall in love again. How did a person do that?

When I got home from work, the light on my answering machine was flashing. I was living on my own, which was expensive. I was in a studio apartment on the first floor of the low-rise where Holly, whom I had gotten to know better, lived with her son.

Her mother and father were dead, and she was the youngest of her five siblings, who were technically half-brothers and half-sisters as three different fathers were involved. There was a picture from the seventies on top of her TV, all the kids with Afros and brightly coloured polyester slacks. "We look like the Jacksons," Holly said. She had come out the lightest because her father was Jamaican-Italian. He had been the caretaker of the building and was sixty-eight when she accidentally arrived. In her own way, Holly was as much a queen bee as Veronika. Some member of her extended family was always visiting; a cousin or foster kid was often crashing on her couch; and there was her girlfriend-but-they-didn't-live-together, Toni.

I checked my voice mail; Dana wanted me to come over. *There's something I need to talk to you about.* That sounded ominous. And she wanted me to go to her apartment? I generally avoided it because Veronika also lived in the building. She owned the property, one of those Parkdale mansions that had been divided into apartments. I hadn't spoken to Veronika since the day I had moved out of our old place, and she had told me she was seeing Lisa. I had even skipped Veronika's mom's funeral, even though by then Dana had informed me Lisa and Veronika were no longer together.

I changed into jeans and left my apartment. It was fall, and the polluted city air was fresh and warm and cool, like slipping a stick of spearmint gum into your mouth. I headed west past Lansdowne to Dana's place in a tonier part of Parkdale. I wouldn't see people like my neighbour who camped out in his wheelchair in the front of our building, drunk or passed out in his own piss, the empty bottles of mouthwash he used to get his buzz on scattered on the sidewalk. As off-putting as he was, I felt equally repulsed by the attitudes of the middle class families who had begun closing in on either side of Parkdale. They had petitioned to shut down a community methadone clinic, which they claimed was a danger to their children. I didn't see how the quiet shuffle of heroin addicts lining up outside the clinic in the mornings was a threat.

"Please don't do that thing with your eyebrows," Dana said, turning from the kitchen counter, where she was standing dishing out cat food into two bowls. Her two cats, Kaspar and Karamel, were weaving between her ankles.

"You just told me you're having a baby with Veronika," I said. "How is that even possible?" Dana had a penis but had told me it was usually soft, that orgasm was difficult to achieve.

"I froze my sperm years ago," Dana explained. "I thought it might come in handy if I had a girlfriend who wanted to have a kid."

I didn't know what to say. When Veronika had occasionally talked about having children, I had thought she said it the way a person said it would be cool to trek in Nepal.

After feeding her cats, Dana presented me with a glass of wine. "Before she died, her mom told Veronika she was worried about her being lonely, that she should have a baby. Vee told her she wasn't lonely, but their conversation made her think seriously about kids."

I sipped the wine. "What about you? Do you want this?" Was Dana lonely?

"I'm super excited about having a baby. I'm sorry I didn't tell you earlier. We didn't think it would happen right away. Anyway, I want you to make up with Veronika. You guys are the two most important people in my life, and I can't stand being in the middle like this anymore." Her voice quavered.

I hadn't thought about how my being mad at Veronika hurt Dana. I stared out the window at the large houses across the street, some of which housed single families and had beautifully landscaped fronts. "Will you be co-parenting?"

"Well, Veronika knows I don't have money to contribute financially, but I'll definitely play a role. We've talked about having me babysit and look after our kid one weekend a month, while Veronika will be the primary caretaker."

Of course she would.

"Look, I know Veronika fucked up," Dana said. "I'm not excusing her, but she was and is going through a tough time, and you did leave Lisa. Also, she had the guts to tell you. Lisa was against that."

"Oh, you don't have to remind me of what an asshole Lisa is."

"Liberty, you hurt me and I forgave you."

I counted in my head while I put on my sneakers. "I didn't *betray* you. I also made a huge effort to work things out. Neither Lisa nor Veronika have taken responsibility for what they did."

I left my drink behind.

The next day as I was leaving work, I was still thinking about my visit with Dana when I heard someone calling my name. It was Beth, the dyke who had been checking my computer.

"Why are you scowling?" she asked as we stepped away from the crowd milling out of the building.

I shrugged. Then I told her the truth. "Boring ex-lover, ex-best-friend shit."

"Ah," she said knowingly, and changed the subject. "Lovely sweater, very Doris Day, of whom I'm a fan."

The sweater was vintage, cashmere from the sixties, turquoise with black trim. Not easy to find. About as easy to find as a Doris Day fan who wasn't a middle-aged gay man.

"Thanks." I blurted out, "Do you want to grab a coffee?" I felt drawn to Beth but wasn't sure I was ready to date.

Perhaps she felt equally unsure about me. She hesitated before saying, "Okay."

We walked for a block until she pointed out a Tim Hortons. I followed her inside and ordered a hot chocolate. I hadn't had one in years, but it was chilly today. Beth ordered a coffee and a maple-glazed donut. While we waited for our order, I took off my glasses and wiped the steam from them.

On our way to an empty table at the back, we passed a group of street kids with baggy pants and neon chokers sharing two cups of coffee and a box of Timbits. The florescent lights made their pale, pimply skin and Magic-Marker hair garish. The kids were talking about infected piercings, and they felt so young to me, no longer a tribe I was part of now that I was edging towards thirty.

I touched a tiny puckered marshmallow floating on the surface of my drink. "I love marshmallows."

From across the table, Beth smiled faintly. "I thought you were the chai latte type."

She was right about what I liked to drink but not about what she thought it meant. I remembered being like the kids sharing the Timbits. I remembered my first week in Toronto, me and Donny on Church Street, standing outside a chain restaurant, looking at the menu and trying to find the cheapest thing on it, which turned out to be apple crisp, and counting our change to split one order. The waiter who had given us the menu said, "For Christ's sake," and took a bill from his change belt and bought us dessert.

I gestured at the street kids. "When I first came to Toronto, I didn't have any money or a place to live." This wasn't something I talked about. It freaked people out, and there was the problem of authenticity, since I was educated and had gotten out of the situation within a few months. Why was I telling Beth?

She said, "Me either. My parents chucked me out for being a dyke, and I lived on the streets for three months. Thank God for the Salvation Army. That's why I give money to them every year, even though they're homophobes."

I was both surprised and not surprised by Beth's admission. Lots of dykes I knew had no relationship or a shitty relationship with their parents. Usually that meant they couldn't bring their lovers home for the holidays and no financial support for things like education or a down payment on a home, but I'd met a few dykes, butches in fact, who had been thrown out of their homes when they were teenagers and wound up working as prostitutes.

"How old were you?"

"Eighteen. I still had a year of high school to go. I got a job in a Chinese restaurant in Brampton and finished up grade thirteen while working thirty hours a week. How about you? Did your parents kick you out for being a dyke?"

I shook my head. "My parents had gay friends. I was more homophobic than they ever were."

She looked puzzled. "So how did you end up without a place to live if your parents were so liberal?"

"I don't quite know."

"Seriously?"

I sighed. I had recently asked my mother why they hadn't helped me, and she'd given me a crap answer about it being a lesson I needed to learn. When I dropped out of school, I think my parents thought I was going to become one of those kids I'd grown up with, almost none of whom made it to university. They couldn't say this because it went against their ideas about equality, their ideas about themselves. But I didn't tell Beth any of this. Instead, I stuck up for my parents.

I said, "I'm not sure they realized how difficult things were for me—my dad always waltzed into jobs." I remembered my father driving Donny and me to the highway so we could hitchhike to Toronto. "Also, there's the fact that in our family hitchhiking and bumming around the country was normal. One of my uncles followed the Grateful Dead for a year, and who knows how he got by? My parents are hippies."

"Really? My family's the type to shoot hippies. Working class, small community, everyone's related. Not quite *Deliverance* but not far from it."

I had grown up among her kind but didn't feel like getting into it. I never talked about Nova Scotia, about growing up. I changed the topic, asked Beth how she knew I was gay. As a femme, my queerness didn't show up on most people's radars. I was out at work but couldn't imagine anyone being sufficiently interested to gossip about it to her.

"There was the whole pronoun thing with 'ex-lover,' and the fact that you asked me to have coffee, but I knew when I met you."

"How could you?"

Beth thought about it for a moment. "You weren't surprised by me."

"You're wrong; I am surprised by you." I warmed my hands on my cup of hot chocolate and noticed I was leaning forward, my body tilted towards her.

I continued. "You know, I haven't thought about being homeless or whatever you want to call it in years. The Salvation Army didn't occur to me. I was hanging out with this guy from Nova Scotia, and at first we crashed in an anarchist house, and then we—well, actually me—took care of some rich gay guy's pets while he was on vacation, and we slept there. Then I met this girl playing chess, you know, on those outdoor chessboards? She kicked my ass at chess and let me stay with her for three weeks. Thank you, Laurie, wherever you are. Then I got a job at a diner, and a waitress I met on my first shift was looking for a roommate."

"A girl who can land on her feet," Beth observed. Her arms rested comfortably on the table, her shirtsleeves pushed up, and I had an impulse to stroke her arm. I noticed her too large men's watch and the time, and Beth saw me noticing.

"Am I keeping you from someone?"

I stood up. "Yes, I totally forgot I have a hair appointment." Holly had suggested that with my curls I should try one of the black hair salons in Parkdale. I had and was pleased with the results.

Beth got up as well. "I'm sorry."

"It's not your fault."

She picked up our cups and napkins. "Which way are you going?"

"West. But I'm going to grab a cab."

"I'm headed east anyway."

The next day, Beth sent me an email with the subject heading "Romance Is Dead" and a web link to the obituary of a world famous romance author who, at the time of her heart attack, was in the midst of her fifth divorce proceeding. *Maybe you should send this to your boss.*

My boss was the obituaries editor. He had a sense of humour, but Princess Di's death had sent him into a tailspin, which I explained to Beth.

She emailed back that her best friend was also in a state of mourning. Her best friend, who was an ex, was strangely obsessed with Princess Di. She had dozens of pictures of her and had applied (unsuccessfully) to be a servant at Windsor Castle when she graduated from high school. *I don't get it.*

I didn't either. Whether a romance with Beth was dead or alive was also unclear. She cancelled lunch plans, and when we grabbed a coffee at work, she mentioned she was newly out of a six-year relationship.

"Six years—that's a long time," I said.

She sighed. "Yeah, I don't know when I'll be ready to date again."

Beth was brushing me off before I had made a move, before I had decided to. I gave her a cool smile. "It was nice having coffee."

For the next month I didn't see or hear from her. She usually worked evenings. I saw her cubicle once on a visit to the IS department and noticed brown cowboy boots were tucked beneath her desk, and a Bruce Springsteen CD was on a shelf above her computer. I was more of a combat-boot-wearing Violent Femmes fan myself. Still, I tucked away the fact that she had been in a six-year relationship. I didn't know anyone who had been in a relationship for that long. Beth struck me as being whatever the opposite of flaky was, and that appealed to me.

Or it would have if Lisa hadn't wrecked me. I was less

angry with her but couldn't tell if it was because I was fed up with being angry or if I'd made progress. I'd recently come to the conclusion that Lisa getting involved with Veronika wasn't the biggest reason I was mad—hell, I could understand that; Veronika was very charismatic. No, what made me mad was how much I missed Lisa. I felt angry and ashamed because I still wanted her while she had "moved on."

Rummaging through a new consignment store in Parkdale, I came across a white shirt made of jersey cotton with a pattern of green seahorses. Men's size small, an Italian designer I had never heard of, too androgynous for me but perfect for Lisa. I wanted to buy it for her and wished she were in my life so that I could. Wanting to dress someone sometimes meant more than wanting to undress them.

I felt a hand on my arm and nearly shouted.

It was Veronika. "Jeez. Sorry. Didn't mean to startle you." She pushed open the shirts on the rack. "Find something cool?"

We hadn't spoken to each other since January. I sometimes spotted her in the neighbourhood and took care to avoid her. I fantasized about yelling at her but never acted on it.

Now I stepped away from the rack. "There's nothing that interesting here." Veronika and Lisa were no longer together but weren't on bad terms. There was no way I would let her get that shirt for Lisa.

Veronika took a deep breath. "I, uh, followed you into the store. I've really missed you. Do you want to have lunch?"

How about an apology? "I have somewhere I have to

be." This was true. I was headed to the Elizabeth Fry Society to set up their archives.

She looked disappointed. I waited to see if she would say anything more when she covered her mouth with her fist. I followed her rapid pace out the door and into the closest alley. Liquid the colour of dark piss arced from her mouth to the ground. She put an unsteady hand on the back of a building.

"So much for lunch," I said. "Morning sickness?"

She nodded and crouched down with her back against the building. I joined her, even though it was cold and windy. Crinkled, rust-coloured leaves and debris from a broken garbage bag whirled by. It was so weird that Veronika was having Dana's baby. Dana was right—under the circumstances, it was impossible for me to ignore Veronika forever.

"I shouldn't have slept with Lisa," Veronika said.

I couldn't meet her eyes. "It kind of devastated me."

"I know. I'm sorry."

My hands fisted inside my coat pockets. Was she truly sorry or saying it because Dana had asked her to? "Why did you do it?"

She tilted her head and rubbed the back of her neck. When she spoke, she sounded tired. "Why do I do anything, Liberty? Because I wanted to, because I don't think about other people enough, because I'm a spoiled only child. Would I do it again? No."

I considered her words. She was being honest. Hadn't used her mother or Claude as an excuse. That was something. "Why aren't you and Lisa still together?"

"My wanting a baby expedited things."

This I could imagine.

"Believe it or not, Liberty, you hurt her."

"Don't tell me that." Don't make me hope.

Veronika read my mind. "She's seeing someone new."

I swallowed. "Why am I not surprised?"

We went across the street to FullWorth. Wandered down the first aisle, past giant burlap bags of rice, black hair products, and stainless steel cookware. Stopped in front of the fridge. Veronika grabbed some ginger beer and paid for it. Outside the store, I told her I had to go.

I went to the office Christmas party in the hope of running into Beth. When I walked into the sports bar, I spotted her at the back. She raised her eyebrows at me and came over. She was dressed up in the manner of butches: dark slacks, pressed white shirt, and hair newly cut and smelling faintly and pleasantly of pomade. Had she got decked out for me? Most people were in jeans or khakis and had come straight from work.

"The craziest thing just happened," she said.

"What's that?"

She gestured to where she'd come from. "I went downstairs to the women's washroom, and this guy followed me in because I guess he thought I was a guy. An older lady, who was washing her hands at the sink, stared at us in complete shock. Then the guy pointed to her and said to me, 'What's that woman doing in the men's toilet?'"

I laughed. "Funny. What did you tell him?"

"Nothing. I went into the stall." She shook her head.

"I hate it when stuff like that happens at work."

Being mistaken for a man had never happened to me, but I got that being queer at work wasn't always comfortable. I usually waited until someone asked if I was married or had a boyfriend before explaining that I was gay. Invariably, a few gaped as though I were performing cunnilingus in front of them. I'd morphed from boring librarian to porn librarian.

Beth took $20 from her wallet, folded the bill, and stuck it on the bar.

I touched her arm. "Drinks are free."

"I didn't know that!"

"Did you just get here?"

"Yeah, about five minutes ago."

The bartender came over, and Beth asked him for a beer. As she waited for her drink, she told me two of her co-workers were dating. "I don't think that's a good idea," she said.

I shrugged. I got the message—she wasn't interested. Disappointing, but she was cool; perhaps we'd become friends. Outside the front window, a streetcar had stopped and crowds swarmed through the front and back doors.

"Are you getting a drink?" Beth asked into the space of my silence.

"Why not?"

When Beth's beer came, I asked the bartender to bring me a gin and tonic. Then I asked Beth why she and her girlfriend had split up.

She hesitated. "She asked me if I still thought of her as a lover, and I told her the truth, which was no, and she told me to move out."

"So officially she dumped you, but she did it because you rejected her."

"I guess." She watched me squeeze my lime into my drink and take a sip. "How about you?"

"The other way around. Officially I dumped her, but she rejected me." I took a sip of my drink. "Let's talk about something besides exes. Are you really a Bruce Springsteen fan?"

She was a fan. Did I understand the brilliance of "Secret Garden," which was about how a woman could sleep with you, love you, without you ever knowing her mind? I had never deconstructed Bruce Springsteen, had barely listened to him, and so demurred. Our differences piled up: While my parents were dragging me to marches for nuclear disarmament, she was in the militia, learning how to use a rocket launcher. Would still be in it or the armed forces if she hadn't been kicked out for being a dyke. Thought unilateral disarmament was naïve and Russia was and always would be the Evil Empire.

At some point, we realized it was really late, that we hadn't talked to anyone besides each other. Beth invited me out for coffee, and I laughed. Here I had given up on her, and she had decided she was interested!

"That wasn't the reaction I was looking for," she muttered.

"Didn't you say something earlier about how colleagues shouldn't date?"

"I was waiting for you to contradict me!"

I folded my arms. "So you were playing games?"

Beth pretended to duck. "I was giving you an out."

"You're too subtle for me."

With less subtlety, she picked up my coat and held it out, and attraction flashed, a sudden fog of it, thick, damp, visceral. I slipped my arms into the sleeves of my coat.

At my place, I made us drinks and put on some trance music. Beth sat as far away from me on the couch as she possibly could. What was going on?

"Are we going to have sex?" I asked.

Beth began to stammer, and I realized she was just nervous. I reached over and took her drink out of her hand and kissed her. Her tongue darted into my mouth before she pulled away.

She said, "I haven't done this in a while. My last relationship was the longest I've gone without sex."

"I see," I said, although I didn't.

Sex began quickly. Beth was in a rush, or at least in a rush to undress me. She put her hand on mine when I began to unbutton her shirt. "I don't want to take off my clothes. I just want to do you."

Inwardly, I sighed. If she'd never let me do her, I didn't want to date her. Now wasn't the time to process this, though.

Beth took off her glasses, and I commented on how long and thick her eyelashes were. "They're beautiful."

She looked pained. "They're always getting stuck together."

Compliments made her uncomfortable. She was insecure but turned out to be a confident lover.

"I've wanted you since the first time we had coffee,"

she confessed as she kissed my belly.

"Hmm." Her touch, her kisses were almost *too* relaxing. I was drunk and sleepy. Had almost nodded off when I registered a teasing lick. I closed my eyes, let the sounds of a sitar drift over me, let her tongue toy with me. My orgasm, when it came, went on and on, my cunt a timpani drum with the skin stretched tight and her mouth the bang of foot pedals striking different places, changing yet never disturbing the tension.

Afterwards, Beth nudged me, hard. "Are you falling asleep? What are you, a guy?"

I blinked. "You said you didn't want to get done."

Beth blushed. "I changed my mind."

I tried not to yawn and obligingly sat up. She was tearing off her clothes, pulling each pant leg over her socks, and then ripping them off as well. Along with her boxers, she had an elaborate underwire bra. When it came off, I saw she had larger breasts than any woman I had been with.

"What size bra do you wear?" I asked.

Beth's mouth dropped open. "You really know how to talk to a girl!"

I spotted her bra on the floor and reached for it, but she was quicker and scooped it up before I could.

I teased, "Wouldn't it be more fun to give in to me?"

She draped the bra over my fingers. Her cup size was double-D, and instinct told me not to say anything more, not even a compliment. Lisa joked about how flat-chested she was, but Beth didn't have her self-assurance.

I cast the bra aside. Got on top of her. Bit her neck and played with her breasts. She groaned and pushed her body upwards, almost throwing me off, not realizing her own strength.

"Sorry, sorry," she said.

"It's okay." I nudged my thigh between hers, and she let her legs fall to either side.

I asked, "Can I lick you?"

"If you like," she said. "I prefer getting fucked."

I fucked her. She bucked against my hand and whimpered. When I thought she might be ready to come, I slowed down and rubbed her clit. The spot where the sensation was sharpest kept shifting, a butterfly I couldn't net. The noise from Beth subsided, so I stopped trying to give her an orgasm and went back to fucking her. Looped and spun her through pleasure until she put her hand over mine and told me she couldn't take it anymore.

When I eased my fingers out of her, Beth kissed my hand. "Thank you," she said.

We spent weekends together. No weekday nights, although we talked every day. We said we were "taking things slow," as though we were following a dating manual rather than being guided by mutual uncertainty. Beth wasn't ready to leap into a new relationship, and I felt panicky over whether I was sufficiently "into" Beth. I had plunged into love with Lisa—this didn't feel the same. But when I stopped worrying about what I felt, what I wanted, being with Beth was a lot of fun.

I brought her to Veronika's shower. On the way over, we talked about kids, which neither of us wanted. Beth adored babies but thought children were annoying. She loved animals and wanted to get a dog as soon as she had a more stable job. Her ex had been allergic.

I said I was scared I'd suck at being a mom.

"I don't think so. You're very protective."

"I am?"

"Yeah. Remember when you went shopping with me, and I got some boxer shorts, and the guy in the store was uncomfortable and didn't want me to try them on? You weren't having any of it. You acted like everything was normal and he was being really weird. And whenever anyone looks at me like they are about to tell me to get out of the bathroom? You glare at them."

I hadn't exactly realized I did this. "Well, I am an older sister, and I hate seeing people treated badly." The idea that I might NOT suck at being a mom was scary. Still, I didn't think I would reproduce. I didn't think my brother would either. He, as some Scotian kids do, had run away to sea. Sailed billionaire's yachts around the world and was getting his captain's papers.

Veronika's apartment was the top floor of the house she had bought. Just beyond the kitchen was a deck, and two of her cousins were outside, smoking. Everyone else was in the kitchen, drinking wine and feasting on a spread that, unfortunately for vegetarian Beth, included a great deal of meat—beef stew, spicy red sausage, peppers and cabbages stuffed with beef and pork and rice, breaded mushrooms, cheese, and zucchinis. Dana gave me a squeeze as we joined the guests discussing Veronika's plan to have a home birth in a wading pool. Her gay male friends and the lesbians present looked squeamish, while her straight female yoga buddies enthused about their own experiences.

Dana asked me, "Did your parents do that?"

"No." I had been born in the United States, where people didn't fuck around with anything their insurance might not cover. "They thought it was too risky."

Veronika said, "My doula says statistically there are fewer risks."

"In Toronto, where you can get your ass to a hospital quickly," Beth pointed out. A few people nodded in agreement.

Veronika patted her belly. "I want to do this naturally."

"Just don't bite off the umbilical cord and eat the placenta," I said.

"I was planning on burying it in Sorauren Park on the first full moon following the birth."

We both laughed. I hadn't entirely forgiven Veronika but hanging out was proving effortless. Later, as the guests filed out and I loaded Veronika's dishwasher, she gestured at Beth's back and whispered, "She's nuts about you."

"How can you tell?"

"When she picked up one of your curls and said it's so many different colours?"

I flushed. "I didn't think anyone heard that."

In March, Beth rented a car, and we drove to Niagara Falls. Around us, the empty fields were frozen with patches of shining snow, and the trees were shorn of leaves, their dark branches framed by a silver sky. The wind through a slit of open window felt wild on my face, and my heart stitched fast in my chest.

When we got there, the falls were covered in snow and ice, a blaze of Arctic whiteness. We stood together in the cold, gazing at the crystalline avalanche before us. I thought about the people who had gone over the falls in barrels and on Jet Skis and died. I looked at Beth, and we embraced tightly and kissed. A man in a car driving by honked at us and waved. I realized he thought we were straight newlyweds.

Beth laughed. "Approval is weird."

"I know."

Even in a big city like Toronto, we got hassled. "Fucking dykes," said the homeless guy begging for change at the corner of Lansdowne and Queen. "Be glad you have someone to feel superior to," I had replied in a cheerful tone, and he hadn't known how to react. This shit happened to us often enough that I could try out and perfect different responses. In the winter, there were fewer incidents—a bulky coat hid Beth's breasts, so she passed for a guy, except that created problems when she used a public bathroom. Last week, a security guard had tackled her.

Now I shivered, and Beth led me back to the car, her gloved hand grasping my mitten. We got take-out veggie burgers and drove back to the city listening to Moby. ("You're making me more sophisticated," she said.)

She told me a story about going camping in a park when she was a teenager and seeing a family run over a rabbit with their car as they roared into the campsite. She had picked up the dead rabbit and tracked down the family and presented the corpse to them. "You killed this rabbit," she said. The two children immediately started sobbing. "Daddy, you said it ran away!" Their father looked stricken, while the mother gave Beth a grim look. She wound up digging a hole and burying the rabbit and having a funeral service with the children.

We laughed until our stomachs hurt. Beth made me laugh more than anyone ever had. She even made me laugh at myself. I felt something I hadn't felt in a long time—happy.

The night before, I had called her at work and asked her to come over and "do" me, and she got offended.

"Is that all I am to you, a good fuck?"

I rolled my eyes. "No! But I do have PMS right now."

"You want me to drop everything and make you come?"

I refrained from reminding her that this was one of her fantasies. After a few seconds, she remarked petulantly, "I'm the girl in this relationship."

I giggled. "Clearly!"

This didn't amuse her, but she did come over. We starting making out as soon as she walked in the door. I was wearing a vintage peach slip and leather harness. The soft leather straps and cool metal buckle of the harness were tightly pressed against my thighs and cunt and ass, and I was already wet. While she began taking off her clothes, I lifted up my slip and fitted my dildo into my harness.

"I bet you want my dick inside you," I told her, emphasizing the word *dick*.

She shook her head. "You're so femme—I can't believe you call it your dick."

"Because there's no such thing as a chick with a dick," I joked. I rubbed lube onto the dildo and waited for Beth to tell me what she wanted.

"Fuck me," she whispered. "I'm ready for it."

I got on top and slid the dildo into her, and she grabbed my buttocks and moaned. As I fucked her, my own cunt ached with the need to come. I jammed my fingers behind my harness and began to play with myself, but it was tricky to fuck Beth at the same time, so I stopped.

"Keep touching yourself," Beth said.

"I'll be doing a sloppy job of fucking you," I protested, even as my fingers almost of their own accord moved over my clit.

"I don't care," she insisted. "Use me."

With those words, I came. Shortly after, she did as well.

The next morning, we both got our periods and laughed about it. Naked, under the sheets, drinking coffee, I told Beth about my first sexual relationship. I was fifteen, and the guy was twenty-six and worked at my parents' store. He never tried to give me an orgasm and told me intercourse hurt because I was young and uptight. I felt yucky without understanding why, without seeing the relationship for what it was: exploitation.

I was equally unable to interpret my attraction to women. In my last year of high school, I went to a women's dance I saw advertised on a poster. Everyone was at least ten years older than me. A woman from Quaker meeting asked me to slow dance, and I did, feeling acutely uncomfortable. Not because she was a woman, but because she was a friend of my parents'. There was a woman wearing a sailor cap that I thought was cute, but she looked so much like a boy I figured that meant I was straight.

I realized I'd been talking on and on. "Sorry! I just wanted you to know that I know what it's like to be used. I would never do that outside of a fantasy."

"I never understood how people couldn't realize they were gay or lesbian. I think I get it now. I used to have perfect hiking vacations with my ex, but our sex life wasn't any good. She giggled when I bought a dildo. Told me she would never use it, that my fantasies of being fucked were wrong, so I shut up about what I liked, did her and didn't let her touch me."

"Why'd you stay with her?"

Beth sighed. "I think I felt guilty. I cheated on my previous girlfriend to be with her, and we were all roommates, so of course it was a total drama. Anyway, I think I had to prove to myself that it was real, that I wasn't some slimy cheater. And I guess I felt weird about what I liked."

"What you like is pretty ordinary," I said. "It's not like I whip you."

"Like you could."

"Oh, is that a challenge?"

I set my coffee down and was about to slap her butt when I felt my wrists being gripped. We tussled and I lost and she slapped my ass.

"You only get to dominate me in the bedroom," she said.

I sat up cross-legged. "Do you really think of me as this big top?"

Beth laughed. "As you would say, hippie girl, it's about energy. You like to be in charge. You do it effortlessly, and it turns you on." She picked up my hand and kissed it. "Having sex with you is like playing paper, scissors, rock. Paper, which seems so easy to tear, covers rock."

"And you're rock?"

"Yup."

She was five years older than me and always telling me things I didn't quite know about myself. Stuff she said was "obvious." Not all of it was good—I was "neurotic," I was "hard" on my friends, on myself—but it didn't feel as though she was going to decide I wasn't worthy. It felt like she was paying close attention. It felt like maybe she loved me.

Later that week, she whispered in my ear that she loved me. We were in the staff lunchroom. "I'm telling you here because you can't run off," she said. "I know you're not ready to hear this."

She was right. I wished she hadn't said it, because I wasn't able to say it back. I felt as if I had the upper hand, and I didn't like it. I also felt like a high-strung thoroughbred being handled by an experienced trainer, a trainer who just might get fed up and auction me off.

On the first truly warm summer night, Beth and I went to see a movie. She was a film buff, so I was surprised by how fidgety she was. I was about to ask her what was wrong when she leaned over and whispered, "I have to go to the hospital."

We left the theatre. Beth was clutching her head. I rushed to the curb and hailed a taxi and told the driver to take us to the nearest hospital.

I turned to Beth. "What's going on?"

"My ears are killing me," she said.

The driver looked at me in his rear-view mirror. "She better not be sick in my car."

I gave him a stern look. "Hurry then."

We stumbled into the brightly lit hospital, and a receptionist took Beth's health care card, and we waited to see the triage nurse. An agitated man with purple hair circled our seats. Not punk but bi-polar. Beth left to go to the bathroom. When she came back, she told me she had thrown up from the pain. She looked pale and I felt scared. Beth's name was called, and I trooped in with her to see the nurse, who wasn't sure what was wrong. They wanted to run tests. She'd probably be spending the night.

"You should go. You have to go to work in a few hours," she said.

She was right, but I didn't want to leave her alone either. "Do you want me to call someone?"

"Like who?"

Beth was a loner. Her best friend was living in Ottawa, and her relationship with her family was fucked up. In community college, she had reached out to them, and things were okay until her brother and sister-in-law sent her a letter telling her their six-year-old daughter had been upset to learn her aunt was a homosexual, and they didn't think it was appropriate for Beth to show up at Christmas with another woman. She could send gifts but not visit. Her parents had defended her brother's decision not to "support Beth's lifestyle."

"I'll stay here," I said. "I'll call my boss, and yours for that matter. I'd like to know you are okay before going home to sleep."

Beth squeezed my hand. "Thank you."

I'd gone home to change, and when I arrived back at the hospital the next day, Beth's parents were there; she had called them. Her father was a big, tall man whose resemblance to Beth was unmistakable; they had the same square face and dark eyes. This could not be said of her tiny mother, who had a face shaped like an apple.

"Mom, Dad, this is Liberty," Beth introduced me. "My partner."

If I was surprised by their presence, they looked even more surprised by me. I recognized the look: *You're a lesbian? You could get a guy.*

I handed Beth some Japanese irises wrapped in paper. The long green stems were formal and elegant while the flowers—a velvety purple striated with lemon and cream— were like floppy hats.

"Lovely," Beth said.

I took a vase from my knapsack and filled it with water from the bathroom sink. As I took the flowers from Beth, I noticed her arm was covered with bruises the size of a fist.

She said, "It's the IV. It's really uncomfortable."

"I'll get the nurse to bring you a different one," I said.

Her father looked nervous. "You don't want to get on their case."

I ignored him and pressed the buzzer and requested an IV line with a smaller needle. A nurse came in and, after a cursory exam of Beth's arm, brought in a new IV line. After she left, Beth's father remarked to me, "Aren't you the bossy Betty!"

"Someone has to look out for Beth," I replied smartly. I turned to my girlfriend. "Have they figured out what's the matter?"

Beth shook her head. "It's kind of mysterious. How did you know I needed a smaller IV?"

"I was a candy striper in junior high."

She laughed. "Really?"

"Quakers are expected to volunteer," I explained. "Listen, I'm going to grab a coffee and let you guys catch up."

Beth's father had goaded me to hide how cowed he was by the authority of nurses and doctors. Probably part of his homophobia was grounded in fear—fear of what would rain down on his daughter for stepping out of line. Understanding this still made his attitude hard to take. Before Beth had come out, he had taught her how to fix things, build things, shoot things; she was praised for being a tomboy, loathed for being a dyke.

When I got back from Starbucks, her parents weren't there, and Beth wouldn't look at me. I sat at the bottom of the bed. "What's going on?"

Beth shifted her legs away from me. "If you're just here because you feel sorry for me, you can leave, too."

"What happened?"

Beth stared at the wall.

I raised my voice. "What did they say?"

She blinked back tears. "I told them, 'I love you,' and my dad didn't say anything, and my mom said, 'I know.'"

My heart pooled in my hand, like a cracked egg. "Well, I love you."

Her fingers curled into her hands, fists clenching her feelings.

"Did you hear me?"

"Your timing sucks," Beth snarled.

When I got home from the hospital, I tried to call Beth, but a nurse told me she was sleeping. I couldn't sleep. I felt like I'd downed three energy drinks. I'd been a withholding jerk, like her homophobic parents. That my reasons were different didn't matter.

What were my reasons? I supposed I was testing her. I didn't want the love Lisa or my parents had for me, which was genuine but no rock I could rest against. My parents had given me some wonderful values and lots of freedom but insufficient protection. Not that they would admit that. But sometimes you have to admit things, say things. It was the only way forward.

At work the next day, I called Beth again but couldn't get through. I did research for my boss on a well-known Canadian architect who was in a coma. The man was nicknamed Flipper, and in an interview he told someone he liked to pretend he was a harp seal, that he wished he were covered in fur. "I go to these conventions where everyone dresses in animal costumes." Was he a furry?

My phone rang, and the call display told me it was Beth.

"Hi," she said.

"How are you?"

"They're letting me out soon with some painkillers. They don't really know why I got such an extreme ear infection."

"That's good news. I mean the part about letting you out."

There was a pause, and Beth asked what I was doing, and I related my research on Flipper. I explained, "There's a coded vocabulary in obituaries. You summarize a life without laying it bare. A fanatic is said to have 'partial views'; a party animal has 'joie de vivre.' I can't think how my boss is going to talk about this furry business though."

"Flipper will be missed by his family and furry friends?" Beth suggested.

"Ooh, I like that!"

We continued chatting until the digits on my phone alerted me to the fact that I'd been talking to Beth for fourteen minutes. "I should get back to it."

"I love you," Beth said. She'd forgiven me. "I love you," I told her. "You have no idea how much." Not saying it hadn't protected either of us. In fact, it had hurt us.

"I know." She said it lightly, without irony.

Play Date

Toronto, 2004

Veronika and her six-year-old son, Elias, were going on a play date with Jiang and her daughter. It maybe could be a real date, but Veronika was trying to be "friends first." When she used to see the phrase "friends first" in lesbian personal ads, she had felt scornful and wondered what women were so afraid of. Was it really a big deal to have sex on the first date? It wasn't as though a woman wouldn't "respect" you in the morning. Now she realized the problem wasn't the next morning; it was waking up three months or six months or two years later and realizing you didn't re-spect your girlfriend.

Besides, the play dates she'd been having with Jiang were fun. Last week, they had gone to The Ex, and the week before, it had been the Toronto Zoo. Today, they were headed to a spa that had a special area for clients' children.

She had met Jiang at a boot camp. Veronika used a scooter to get to class while Jiang drove up in a Lexus SUV. Absorbing her short hair, polo shirt with a popped collar, thick raver-boy necklace, and one-handed push-ups, Veronika heard her gaydar ping. Then she saw Jiang's feet as they changed after class: Her toenails were covered in hot-pink polish. Each toenail visible in her Naot sandals was perfectly buffed and trimmed. She'd had a pedicure. No butch Veronika knew got pedicures. Had Jiang not come out yet? Her Chinese background might mean her family wasn't accepting; on the other hand, Veronika knew exactly one lesbian (Liberty) whose family had had a normal reaction, which is to say none, so maybe Jiang wasn't gay.

Veronika had come out in boot camp when their instructor, a gay man, made a comment that presumed all ladies present were hot for Brad Pitt. "I'm more into his girlfriend," Veronika had piped up. She wasn't, but he got the point and hopefully so did Jiang. She didn't care about the rest of the class, some of whom chimed in with I'm-liberal-and-cool comments about the most-beautiful-woman lists Angelina Jolie topped.

Her coming out didn't spur a reaction in Jiang, who didn't speak to anyone as they jogged around the park, lifted weights, and did squats and jumping jacks. A Chinese guy appeared one day in the SUV with a kid who called Jiang "Mom," so Veronika figured her gaydar had malfunctioned. Not that she was super invested in Jiang being a dyke. Trying to figure her out just made doing core training less tedious.

The week before the course ended, Veronika saw Jiang's toenails were blue with silver sparkles. "Nice toenail polish."

Another woman in their class glanced at Jiang's feet. "Sparkles—that's so fun."

Jiang nodded silently.

As Veronika was scooting home, a car horn sounded. It was Jiang, offering her a lift. As she hoisted Veronika's scooter into the trunk, Jiang said that the only reason she wore toenail polish was because of her daughter. "Sophia likes us to do the same things."

Veronika smiled. So Jiang was gay! And she felt the need to defend her butchness! How cute. What Jiang didn't realize was Veronika didn't care if she wore toenail polish—she'd just been trying to get her attention. "Well, that explains it. I just thought you weren't following the dyke playbook."

That made Jiang laugh. "You're funny." She sounded surprised.

Techno with a brutal beat thumped out of the car stereo, and Veronika said, "This sounds like bombs dropping."

"Exactly."

Turned out Jiang was into the techno-rave scene. Not so much the drugs, though she did like ecstasy. She was twenty-seven, had an eight-year-old daughter, worked as a pharmacist, and was single. She had just had a boring sushi date with a woman she met online, and a hot woman with a boyfriend was messaging her to have a threesome.

Was Jiang signalling she wanted to be friends or letting it be known she was available? Veronika had been out of the game too long to tell. While she was pregnant, she'd been a horny bunny demanding to be fisted, which wasn't a problem—a surprising number of dykes wanted to have sex with a pregnant woman. Then Elias arrived, and the lovers stopped. She was absorbed with her son, glutinous with love, cooing Hungarian endearments, not sleeping much, and constantly nursing, which had felt more industrial than natural and turned her nipples into festering wounds, another reason not to bother with sex.

Fast-forward a few years and hello, Shadow!—punk dog walker. Points for not being a hot cop who wanted to be

Daddy inside and outside the bedroom and didn't get that Dana wasn't just a sperm donor. Nope, Shadow had passed those tests—she doted on Elias and respected Dana—but flunked another one. Shadow didn't want to *be* Mommy; she wanted *a* Mommy. She wanted to be adopted, to never leave the sanctuary of Veronika and Elias's apartment, and that got to be a drag, because there were only so many pizza-and-kid-movie nights a girl could stand, plus their sex life was yawn. When Veronika dumped her, Shadow cut off contact and Elias cried for months, asking for her.

Losing people when you were a kid really hurt. And when it didn't have to happen? When it wasn't cancer? That sucked. Elias deserved better, which meant Veronika had to be careful whom she let into his life. And while Shadow was wrong to punish Elias, maybe Veronika should have been nicer to her? That was the problem with not being nice—people weren't nice back.

A year rolled by, and she made getting into shape her New Year's resolution. Took up tango classes in the winter, Pilates in the spring, and had just finished a summer boot camp course. Liberty told her she was gearing up for her next girlfriend.

"I'm not," Veronika protested, wondering why she wasn't mentioning Jiang. Usually, she loved telling Liberty about her crushes and seductions, but something held her back. The two of them were at a new cupcake store at the end of Queen Street West. Liberty was picking up red velvet vegan cupcakes for Beth, who was now her wife.

Outside the store, they passed a rockabilly bar that used to be a sports bar. Walking into it was a girl in a corset with tattoos like bright murals covering her arms. Girls in

Parkdale no longer worked the streets; they just dressed as though they did. Not that Veronika thought that was a problem; she just didn't have the energy for it herself. Her long dark-brown hair was pulled into a simple ponytail, and she was wearing skinny jeans with a hoodie.

She and Liberty headed over to the Sorauren Farmers' Market to meet up with Dana and Elias. That was what fun was now. Not dancing in a club but watching Dana dance with Elias to a Salvadoran band with flutes. Waiting in line to buy easy-to-heat-up meat pies from Mennonite farms, or purchasing marinated tofu steaks while a white guy with dreadlocks standing beside them demanded to know whether the tofu was GMO-free.

"Goddamn hippie," Liberty said without hostility after they sat down on the grass.

Veronika scrolled through messages on her BlackBerry. "Expecting an email?"

"Looking for a tenant." Veronika rolled her eyes. "The responses are depressing."

She showed the first few to Liberty. The first, all in lower case, said: *two brothers need place after mother passed.* A second, also in lower case, said: *ima full time personal trainer and inyerested in viewing this apartment. im working on the days your showing it.* A third email displayed the user name as sexymama_21 and said: *When can I see it?*

Liberty handed back the BlackBerry. "Parkdale's still pretty rock and roll below King. Who's moving out?"

"Dallas."

Dallas—aka the bad-girl-everyone-wants-to-fuck—was using a male pronoun now and had turned out to be not so bad. Kind of traumatized in fact. He'd been abused and grown up in foster care and suffered from PTSD and was on disability. As a tenant, he caused no problems and paid the rent on time. Unfortunately, he was moving to Whitby with a new girlfriend who had three kids. Veronika suspected he, like Shadow, was looking for an instant family.

"Shit. Speaking of exes." Liberty pointed to the edge of the park. Lisa was jogging around the track with another woman. "I haven't seen or heard anything about her in years!"

Veronika smiled. "She and her partner just bought a house in High Park. I got an invite to their house warming. I can't believe you guys still don't speak to each other."

"You've observed that before," Liberty said coolly. She was the grudge-holding queen.

"Observed what?" Dana asked as she joined them.

Before Veronika could reply, Elias had flung his arms around her legs. "Mommy!" She kissed his cheeks until he squirmed away. He smelled so good. Kids didn't get that sweaty. She loved him like crazy; even when she was bored as she was now listening to him recount his day.

Last year, she had tracked down her high school girlfriend Sharon, who also had kids via her formerly straight partner. Veronika had pushed Sharon and her partner, Nadia, into having lunch. Elias, whom Veronika had brought with her on the road trip to her former hometown, had been a partial icebreaker. Sharon chatted easily about her sons but not about anything else. Mind you, Sharon never had been much of a talker. Dana, who had also accompanied them, learned more from Nadia. While an introvert, working in retail meant Dana knew how to draw people out. On the drive home, Veronika had discovered that Sharon worked at a factory in the automotive industry, and Nadia's ex-husband was her supervisor, and that Nadia and Sharon had been together for over a decade. *Could Sharon and I have lasted?* Probably not—Veronika would have fucked it up by fucking around.

Jiang was in that fucking around phase. She'd gotten pregnant after a fling with a childhood friend when they were on ecstasy and wound up marrying him. Then she fell in love with their Filipino nanny. Now the three of them had condos in Liberty Village, a slightly twisted it-takes-a-village model of raising a kid. According to Jiang, her ex-girlfriend was the best parent. Jiang worked too much, and her ex-husband did too many drugs.

In the locker room of the spa, Elias flung open the locker doors. Having a boy child had been an education in the role of nature and gender differences. He was always energetically pounding and pushing any movable object and was obsessed with trucks and wanted to drive a garbage truck when he grew up.

"Elias, stop it! You're driving me crazy," Veronika said firmly. She despised the moms in Elias' school who lived in upscale neighbourhoods to the west of Parkdale, and pleaded pathetically with their boy children to stop misbehaving.

"Mommy, I'm not." Elias clutched her around the middle.

Veronika picked up his fists and kissed them. "We're going to the kids' area where someone is going to look after you and Sophia. There's a water slide. You'll like it." Hopefully.

The spa Jiang had brought them to was like nothing Veronika had ever seen. The interior reminded her of a high-end condo. Soaring ceilings, skylights, brick walls, and a floor covered in grey and blue ceramic tiles. In addition to the separate facility for kids, there was a massage station, a juice bar, two saunas, and two pools—a small circular one and a large rectangular one full of sea salt. Veronika eased her body into the warm, salty water. This morning, she had debated what to wear: a sexy bikini or a basic black one-piece that hid her stretch marks? She'd opted for a white crocheted bikini. Jiang had stretch marks, too.

They floated together, their elbows on the pool ledge, legs thrust out, idly pumping the water. How long had it been since she'd relaxed? She lurched from work (four days a week but still) to being a mom to being a landlady. By ten, sleep descended.

"Feel good?"

"Feel great!"

"Thought you'd like this place." Jiang glided past Veronika, smoothly pushing her body through the water like a frog. Jiang was neither boyish nor curvy—she had a medium-sized build and graceful moves. The pool filled up, and Jiang suggested they check out the other one.

Veronika plunged into the round pool and screamed. The water was freezing. Jiang stood at the top of the steps, laughing, and Veronika seized her legs and tugged her in. Jiang fought back by splashing icy water at her. They were roughly the same size and evenly matched. They wriggled out of the pool.

"I thought you knew how this worked. You're supposed to get hot, then cold." Jiang pointed to the saunas. "Dry, then wet."

Veronika clutched her arms. How this worked. She didn't have a clue how relationships worked or what she and Jiang were doing let alone how to do the spa right. What was it her mom used to say about Hungarians? They go through a revolving door behind you and come out ahead. She was tired of revolving through relationships. And if always making sure she wasn't the soft one squashed in the door wasn't protecting her, what would?

"Let's warm up." Jiang had forgotten her towel, and her baggy black shorts and red tank top were dripping with water.

Within moments, the heat in the sauna dried their skin. A crocheted bikini in a sauna turned out to be a terrible idea. Veronika desperately wanted to take it off but felt self-conscious. Kids ruined your body. She was thin again, but her boobs weren't something she confidently flashed these days. Fuck it. Reaching around, she undid her bikini top. Stood up and pulled down her bottoms.

Two women in towels got up and left, as though Veronika had broached protocol by undressing. She childishly stuck out her tongue at their retreating backs and grabbed the lower bench they'd been sitting on, which was wider and more comfortable. The hard wooden slats heated her back while she breathed in the sharp, pleasant cedar smell. As she closed her eyes, she felt an ache radiate between her legs. If Jiang touched her, Veronika would let her do whatever she wanted. Spread her legs and not care who saw them. Wait, she would care if Elias and Sophia showed up. That did it, boner killer.

She rolled onto her stomach and told Jiang her high

school girlfriend had just included her in a group email of photos of her twin boys' graduation from middle school.

"You had a girlfriend in high school?"

"Uh-huh. Did you know you liked girls in high school?" She and Jiang hadn't exchanged their coming-out stories.

"Not really," Jiang said. "I was a nice Chinese girl, and I guess I was too scared to think about it. I lost my virginity to a boy I liked and thought, 'This sucks; I must be frigid.' At my wedding, my closeted-but-we-all-knew-he-was-gay cousin asked me if I was *sure* I was making the right decision, and I thought, 'He thinks I'm gay.' Then I asked myself, 'Am I?' Tala was my first." Tala was the nanny who became Jiang's lover. "And you weren't frigid with her?"

"I was a nympho with her."

Veronika didn't want to hear about it, which was funny, because she wasn't the jealous type. She even liked Jiang's ex-girlfriend, who was sweet and had a new partner. "How come you guys broke up?" She sensed it was Jiang who had ended the relationship.

"She's not ambitious. She just liked to make me happy, and somehow that didn't make me happy."

"I don't know how ambitious I am," Veronika said. "I've had the same job for more than ten years."

"Do you like your job?"

"Yeah, but I'm bored. What I love doing is throwing dyke parties, but I can't make a living at it. Dykes don't go out enough."

"What about being a promoter or a special-events co-ordinator?"

"I've never thought of that." It wasn't a bad idea.

Veronika noticed Jiang staring at her, and instantly she

was back to sex, as though the conversation they'd been having hadn't happened. Above her, the bench creaked as Jiang dropped down to stand over her. She slowly stroked Veronika's ass.

"We can't do this here," Jiang said as she continued to touch Veronika. "You need to put your bathing suit back on."

Veronika swallowed. There was a gush of wetness between her legs. "My bathing suit isn't comfortable. Can you, um, get my towel instead? I left it by the pool."

"Sit tight."

The air flowing in as Jiang exited the sauna was cool and refreshing on Veronika's hot, damp skin. When had she last wanted someone this badly?

Jiang returned with the towel. "Do you want to try the wet sauna now?"

Wet–don't even say that word to me. Veronika wrapped the towel around herself. "Okay."

"You won't be able to stand it for long," Jiang warned.

No one was in the wet sauna, which, like the ice water, was almost unbearable. Full of clammy steam that made it hard to breathe. Like doing hot yoga, which Veronika had tried once and hated. She wanted to bust open the door. Jiang kissed her, and Veronika absorbed the kiss. When she felt Jiang's hand skate between her legs, she didn't know whether she was going to faint or have an orgasm. *I am melted and destroyed.* She gestured at the door, and Jiang released her.

Outside, Veronika's knees buckled. She fell into a pleather lounge chair the colour of a lime-green Popsicle. Jiang brought her a cloudy drink that was sweet and hot.

"What is this?"

"Raw sugar cane with cayenne and ginger. It's supposed to cleanse you."

It seemed to work. After a minute, Veronika felt calmer. Jiang was sitting cross-legged in front of her. A lock of wet hair had fallen onto Jiang's forehead, and Veronika swept her hair from her face, one of those mom gestures she naturally did now.

"So," Jiang said.

"So."

"Am I too young?"

This had never occurred to Veronika, who rather liked the idea of being a cougar, though there wasn't enough of an age discrepancy between them for that. "No, it's Elias. I have to consider what's best for him. I can't just get into a relationship."

Except she already had.

Parkdale II

Toronto, 2007

Dana strode in and out of the boutiques that had bloomed along Queen, leaving flyers about the closing of Curious. The owners of an art gallery, the conspiracy store that sold organic weed, and the place that ran knitting workshops all said the same thing: "Tough to make a living when rent and property taxes are through the roof." She didn't bother explaining her bosses were simply retiring. It was strange to think she would be out of work in less than two weeks. She hadn't lined up another job. The past year had been too fraught for her to take it on.

In January, she'd finally had genital reconstruction surgery. It hadn't gone smoothly. She developed an infection and was in the hospital for two weeks, and the post-op process of stents and dilating her new vagina was gruelling and painful. Her pee sprayed all over the toilet for months, messy and gross, not to mention ironic. She felt like the Little Mermaid getting legs that looked beautiful and made her feel as though she were walking on knives. She dragged her ass to work three days a week and otherwise stayed in with her cats, watching reality television shows about models.

By the summer, her regimen had paid off and now her vagina was fine. More than fine—she'd discovered she could have orgasms, which inspired her to post a personal ad, her first attempt in many years to enter the dating world. Sadly, it hadn't been successful.

As she stepped into a neighbourhood bar, she spotted Holly. An event was going on. Women were unpacking giant platters of finger foods and desserts and setting them out on tables. Didn't this place serve food?

Dana approached Holly. "Hey, what's happening?" She held out a flyer to Holly, who barely glanced at it.

"It's a BBW event."

"A what?"

Holly looked uncomfortable, which was unlike her. Though she had a critique of how society positioned black women as Fabulous, she also was that poised, stylish fag hag. "It's a Big Beautiful Woman event."

The size of the women around Dana swam into focus. They were mostly obese and a tad suburban in oversize bedazzled T-shirts and drapey dresses. Holly, in a black and white polka dot dress, was the only urban fashionista and the only black woman, though there were some black men. Was this where Holly met her sexual partners? After she split up with her long-term girlfriend, Toni, she'd been spotted with a succession of young guys.

"Your eyes are popping out," Holly said.

"Sorry," Dana apologized. "See anyone here you fancy?"

"Besides you, darling? No." Holly glanced at a black man with dreads the size of ball pythons and lowered her voice. "He just told me, 'I'll be your lover, baby.' Points for directness, except he's a dead ringer for my cousin Sammy, and sleeping with him would feel like incest."

"What did you do?"

"Introduced him to Kelly." Holly gestured with her chin

to the white woman standing beside him. She was pushing down a red corset to show him a tattoo on her breast.

"Looks like it worked out."

Holly smiled. "Um hm. Feel like getting something to eat?"

"If it's free, I should take advantage, seeing as I'll be out of a job soon." She was hungry, and the homemade Nanaimo bars looked inviting. They picked up plates and got into line.

"Why is this event here?" Dana asked as she selected some chips. The Nanaimo bars had disappeared. Some women ahead of her in line had loaded up on the decadent desserts while other women sat at tables, drinking water and not eating a thing.

Holly put a scoop of potato salad on her plate along with some olives and cold cuts. She was a savoury person. "The manager of the bar is an FA."

Dana asked, "A what?"

"Fat admirer. Don't you ever read Craigslist or personal ads?"

"I put one up recently," Dana admitted. "It was a mistake."

On her ad, she had put it out there that she was a gay trans woman who had just had gender reassignment surgery, hoping to stem responses from men or hostile lesbians. She didn't hear from any hostile lesbians but received forty emails from men and only three from women. The first woman didn't state her sexual orientation (desperate, Dana concluded) and wrote: *I have two kids that drive me insane most days. I have cronic pain and smoke weed to help.* The next response came from a woman who had just gotten out of a relationship. Her handle was Left Numb, which sounded fucked up, but her Suicide Girl photo was very attractive and she'd dated at least one trans woman. However, their Starbucks coffee date hadn't gone well. Dana had the same name as the woman's ex, so the woman called her "Good Dana," and her ex, to whom she made copious references, was "Bad Dana." "I think I can do better," Dana had told Liberty afterwards. "Dying alone with your cats would be better," Liberty had replied.

That date was followed by one with a trans woman. She was kind of butch, but Dana had tried to be open. Over dinner at a chain restaurant, the woman had talked non-stop about a house she had bought and insisted Dana watch a ten-minute video on her phone of the home inspection. While the woman went to the bathroom, Dana had texted Veronika: *Every dyke I meet who is single is either boring or broken.* Veronika had texted back: *Let's not forget boring and broken.* Of course, it was easy for Veronika and Liberty to be snarky: They both had partners.

Holly led them to a table in the corner, away from the others. Women and a few men greeted her and seemed willing to make space at their tables. When Holly didn't join them, they looked Dana over as though she were Holly's date. It was funny because she'd never considered dating Holly. She'd always found her intimidating.

Over food, they chatted about Holly's son, Dominic, who had just been laid off from his warehouse job.

"I'm worried about him because he's not a focused in-dividual. My family are all, like, 'Why are you up in his business. He's been working since middle school.' They don't get that it's a problem not to have a capital-P plan or a capital-P passion."

The same could be said of Dana. She had no future plans beyond EI and selling jewelry on eBay, and her post-secondary education consisted of an unfinished degree from the Ontario College of Art and Design.

"Is that the worst thing?" Dana asked. "When I was his age, I was just trying to figure out who I was. My big plan at the end of high school was to live in Toronto and find a wild artist girlfriend who lived in a loft."

"Yeah, well, white kids mostly land on their feet. Black boys not so much." Holly scraped up the last of her potato salad with her plastic fork and chewed thoughtfully. "At least that's the big picture. The smaller picture is Dominic's father has promised to get him a job as a bartender at an after-hours club, and who knows what business happens there?"

This was news. Holly never talked about the gay man who had been her boyfriend for her entire adolescence and into her adulthood. She wouldn't even use his name; he was simply "Dominic's father." Clearly, there were issues, though what they entailed was a mystery.

"I didn't know Dominic was in contact with his dad."

"His dad was in the States for years. Now he's back in Toronto and wants to do the father–son thing seeing as Dominic's grown and he doesn't have to worry about support payments. I'm staying out of it, letting Dominic figure out for himself who his daddy is."

Dana couldn't keep from prying. "And who is he?"

Holly gave Dana a look. A look that said, "I'm tolerating your question because I like you, and because I'm curious as to why Miss Shy-and-Polite is asking." Dana wasn't sure what instinct was making her push Holly, who was a blunt yet private person. Not only was there the mystery of Dominic's father but also of Holly's other relationships. No one knew exactly why she and Toni had split. Toni famously never left her apartment, and Holly referred to unspecified mental health problems, but even Veronika and Liberty, who were very direct, hadn't dug out the whole story.

Holly sighed. "Dominic's father is a man for whom every relationship is a hustle, is about what the other person can do for him."

Which explained a lot and also nothing.

A woman approached their table. She was an acquaintance of Holly's and was what Dana's mother would have called "a chatty Cathy." Her name was Stacy, and she vented about her ex-boyfriend, who was wolfing down a plate of nachos at the bar. This guy, like most of the women there, was very large, and she said she'd met him at a previous BBW gathering. "He's afraid I'm going to steal his nachos," the woman said. "Go back to your hotel room, asshole, and jerk off by yourself then." He was from Niagara Falls; she was from Barrie.

"Holly's from Toronto, but most of us aren't," Stacy said. "That table over there?" She gestured at a group of loudly laughing women. "They rented a van and drove up from Michigan."

These women were all holding bottles of water, and Stacy noticed Dana noticing this and explained they'd had gastric bypass surgery and couldn't eat much of anything.

The room was emptying out. Stacy drifted to another table, and Holly said she was ready to go. "I'll walk you home," Dana said.

Outside, the temperature was unseasonably warm for

October. A new window-serve taco bar owned by a celebrity chef had opened next door. Although it was almost nine o'clock, people were standing in line, waiting for tacos with unlikely ingredients—eel, braised beef, tofu and jicama. The tall, narrow building housing the taco joint was covered in a bright Mexican-style mural and was one of several new restaurants on Queen Street.

Parkdale had become a destination neighbourhood. The giant apartment buildings continued to be inhabited by immigrants and poor folks, but on street after street, house after house was being bought and tastefully renovated by people who could afford to throw down tens of thousands of dollars on upgrades. Not a possibility for Dana, even ten years ago when houses were cheap and the rent on a basement apartment could cover a mortgage—her money had gone towards her body, to hair removal and surgeries.

"I can't believe Curious is closing," Holly said. She, too, seemed to be thinking about the changes to their neighbourhood. "I've been getting my jewelery there forever."

"The first time I met you, you were buying polka dot earrings."

"You were such a sweetheart. I had no money, no credit card, and you let me buy them on layaway with no deposit. I'd come by every two weeks and put down ten dollars."

Dana glanced up, and she and Holly smiled at each other. They continued down Queen towards Holly's apartment in a companionable silence. As they waited at the light to head north, Holly began talking about the event they had left.

"The scene's a little messed up. You've got some eating-disorder action, women who don't eat and women who eat too much."

Dana remembered how all the Nanaimo bars had disappeared and a table of women who each had multiple desserts in front of them.

Holly continued, "Some of it is binge eating, and some of it is for the guys who get turned on watching women eat. I wouldn't date one of those guys, but I like being able to eat a full plate of food and not get the stinkeye from every non-fat person in the room. I also like—and I get that this is fucked up—not being the biggest woman in the room."

Dana blinked. She had this idea that black women weren't as concerned as white women were about having a big body. "This is probably a sweeping statement, but isn't size less of an issue in the black community?"

Holly sighed. "Yes and no. I mean there are black guys who are all 'I like my women thick,' but a couple weeks ago this West Indian cab driver refused to let me in his cab because I was eating a donut. He told me, 'Woman, you fat enough already.'"

"That is so fucked up!" Dana said.

Why had she and Holly never had this conversation before? Probably for the same reason she didn't talk to her friends about peeing all over the toilet. You didn't want them to feel sorry for you. You didn't want to take the chance they would say something stupid and hard to forgive.

Dana stepped off the Lansdowne bus and walked through the parkette at the end of West Lodge. Groups of young Tibetan men in saggy pants sat in circles on the ground, playing sho. There was a constant thwunk as the boys slammed the bowl over the dice. Impulsively, she sat on a swing. Maybe because Holly was on her mind, she found herself watching a just-hitting-puberty black girl climb up the slide. Just outside the park, she noticed two cops questioning some black youth.

In some ways, Dana thought, the world never changed. In other ways, it did. Last week, she and Elias were watching an episode of *Veronica Mars* in which the girl detective was hired to find a boy's father who turned out to be a trans woman. When the show ended, Elias said, "I don't understand. Why is the boy upset his dad is a lady?" Dana had smiled. "Because he doesn't live in Parkdale."

Dana loved Parkdale. The new percolated here. If she'd been willing to live on a goat farm, she might still be with her two ex-girlfriends. She'd met them at Hillside Festival, where she was selling jewelry, and they were selling goat's milk soap, and their first year and a half together had been wonderful. By the third year, their poly triad had metastasized into a quad that eventually imploded. A cisgender male WWOOFer (willing worker on an organic farm) had shown up, and one of Dana's girlfriends hooked up with him. She had used poly as a way to avoid breaking up with her girlfriends ("I'm just putting my energy over here right now.") Not that Dana was one of those bitter people who said poly couldn't work just because her situation hadn't.

It *had* worked for a couple years. Veronika hadn't been thrilled about Dana taking Elias away on weekends, but he'd loved the farm. It had been cool to teach Elias about plants and animals and pests and tools and machinery and how to grow vegetables. Things Dana couldn't show Elias at his grandparents' since Dana's contact with her family was limited to an annual visit from her sister and father that occurred in Toronto in early December. She suspected they didn't share the news of these visits with Dana's mother and her sister's religious nut of a husband.

People like her brother-in-law were the reason Dana didn't want to live full-time in a community where there were no trans folks and they were the only queers. Her lovers had countered that in a farming community what mattered was who helped out in a storm. To an extent that was true but only to an extent. Also, Dana hadn't wanted to farm, to work that hard every day, to watch animals die, to always be filthy and live in boots and overalls. In overalls, she wasn't sure she could pass, and she hated that.

She got off the swing and started walking home. Thoughts of Holly swam through her head. Ever since the Big Beautiful Woman night, she'd been thinking about her friend differently. Was in fact crushing on her. Was it because the night had opened a window onto Holly's vulnerability that made her seem more accessible? Perhaps, but the idea seemed a bit fake, like something from a romance novel.

They had been friends forever. Holly dropped by Curious every few months and was always a guest at the elaborate birthday parties Veronika arranged for Elias, including the really unfortunate one where a mobile petting zoo had been booked. But it was a friendship with a whiff of other possibilities—Holly always kissed Dana's cheek when they saw each other and didn't do that with their other friends. *She flirts with me in this practiced, casual way that I pretend not to notice but have always secretly enjoyed.* But on the night Dana had walked her home from the BBW event, Holly hadn't reached out and given her the usual goodbye hug. And because she hadn't, their goodnight had been strained in a way Dana intuited was a surprise for them both. "You take care," Holly had said without looking at her. After a slight hesitation, Dana echoed, "You, too."

On the web, Dana had read about a trans woman who'd just had GRS and was auctioning off her virginity on eBay, something she couldn't imagine doing. Holly on the other hand was someone she trusted to test-drive her new parts. *Maybe my feelings have changed because I've changed; maybe I'm willing to go there now because Holly, who actually likes penises, can't treat me like I'm part boy if I have a vagina.*

Maybe it was time to ask Holly out on a date.

It was nine o'clock on a Saturday evening, and Dana was pacing back and forth. Her apartment was sparkling clean, and there was a bottle of expensive white wine in the fridge. Not that she was even sure she could drink. She was so nervous she felt as if she might throw up, even though the person she was waiting for was her long-time friend.

Oh! There went the doorbell. She buzzed Holly in and took her black leather coat and hung it up in the closet. Offered to take her giant purple handbag but Holly smiled and shook her head. The velour tracksuit she was wearing was the same vivid purple as her handbag, and looked easy to slip out of, which was the point of this evening that Dana had arranged with a series of tentative *you-can-totally-reject me-if-you-want* emails. Except that Holly hadn't rejected her.

"Would you like some wine?" Dana asked. "I have a Chardonnay and an ice wine in the fridge, or there's some Pinot Noir if you prefer red."

"The Chardonnay sounds good."

Dana managed to uncork the bottle and pour the wine. Holly began thumbing through Dana's massive collection of LPs from the seventies. Liberty said the only male thing left in Dana was her vinyl collection, in particular her Journey, Boston, and ELO records.

"Do you have any hip hop?"

"Um, no."

Holly squealed as she pulled out a Dionne Warwick album. "I love Dionne! My mom had all her records. But that's hurting music, too sad for tonight."

"I have Sirius radio for another month," Dana said. "How about some deep house?"

"That works."

Dana set the station. When she'd finished, Holly lifted her wineglass in the direction of Dana's bedroom. "Let's go."

The raison d'être for the large handbag was revealed. Holly liked toys. Vibrators, dildos, and what looked like a butt plug were spilled across Dana's bed. She counted four dildos: a black silicone one, a white plastic one with a gold metal band, a glass dildo, and a lavender feminist dolphin also made from silicone. Did Holly expect her to strap it on? She must. Dana had hoped to use her fingers, her tongue.

"Among other things, I'm a sex-toy virgin," Dana said. She was sitting in Holly's lap, facing her. Holly's legs were spread flat—she was limber and flexible; she did judo—and their pussies were pressed together through their respective sweatpants and leggings. They had been making out until Holly reached over and upended her bag.

Holly cocked an eye. "You've got to have a vibrator."

Dana shook her head. "Nope."

The object closest to them looked like a double-headed hair dryer, and Holly lifted it up for Dana to see. "This vibrator is for two, and it feels pretty great. If you decide to get one, skip the battery-operated ones and go right for the plug-ins."

Dana kissed Holly to make her stop talking like a feminist sex educator. They rocked against each other, and Holly rubbed her boobs back and forth across Dana's chest, producing a steady buzz of sensation in her vagina. At least until Holly flipped her on her back and arranged her legs in some way that she couldn't move. It made Dana want to come, which was strange—she was used to just pleasing her partners.

"Do you want me to fuck you now?" Holly batted her eyelashes at Dana.

"I want you to touch me." The pressure of Holly's large body ceased, and Dana had an acute feeling of loss. She realized Holly was waiting for her to undress. She took off her socks and leggings and black dress and lacy pink bra and underwear. Presented herself like a gift to Holly, who spread Dana's legs and began playing with her, teasingly pressing here and there. It felt amazing. In her head, Dana chanted, "Oh, Holly, Holly, God, Holly." Out loud, she managed to gasp, "I'm not as flexible, and I don't get wet."

"I figured," Holly said. "Do you want lube?" She handed over a tube.

"Yeah."

Lube was so goopy and sticky but made coming easier. While Dana squirted lube onto her palm and rubbed herself, Holly surveyed the toys. After a moment, she selected a not-too-intimidating white and pink electric vibrator and a very intimidating butt plug.

The first toy was plugged into an outlet and wielded on Dana, who within minutes felt her cunt pop with a tiny orgasm. She barely had a chance to recover when she felt Holly guide her onto her knees and put one hand over her pussy as though she were holding it in place and the other hand in the crack of her ass. More lube, a finger, and eventually the scary toy entered her. She didn't feel anxious about it. Thought had dissolved. Her body was a shooting star, metal and rock falling into the atmosphere to become streaking, exploding light.

Stepping Out

Toronto, 2010–2011

Beth's body was erupting with pain, mostly in her knees. Arthritis, a doctor said, except it was unusual for someone her age to have such an advanced case. She was put on a long waiting list for knee replacement surgery, and the doctor told her it would be better for her not to work, but we couldn't afford it. She did contracts until the pain got too bad. I'd come home from my job—a contract cataloguing books about the history of footwear at a shoe museum because before all this had gone down I'd decided I was sick of working on Bay Street—and she'd be on our bed, rocking and crying for hours and hours. Tough to watch and worse to go through. Eventually, I'd go downstairs and make supper and sleep on the couch. I couldn't do anything for her besides pay our bills. I couldn't take her pain away. No gentle cloth pressed to her forehead, no soothing touch—my touch hurt her. Even just holding her hand. Everything hurt her.

We had the following conversation a number of times:

Her: I'm so sorry. (Unspoken but understood: for being in pain, for losing my temper because I'm in pain, for being a drag, for not being able to have sex.)

Me: It's not your fault. I think you are handling it as well as you can.

Her: I wouldn't blame you if you left. (Yeah, right.)

Me: There was this thing I took called a marriage vow? You know, for richer or for poorer, in sickness and in health. I didn't miss the fine print. Besides, what if I got MS? Would YOU leave?

Her: (Feeble smile.) I'd be off like a shot. (More serious expression.) You can look elsewhere for sex, you know. (It had now been a year and a half.) I just don't want to hear about it, okay?

Me: Um, okay.

I missed having sex. I missed having sex with her. But coming home to the pain show every night just made me too sad to want to do much of anything.

Then. Morphine. A game-changer. Beth slept a lot, and I felt like I could breathe again.

Then. Diamond. After almost a decade in Vancouver, Veronika's ex and my one-time crush had returned to Toronto. She invited me to be her Facebook friend, and a few emails led to a drink together in a bar.

As the afternoon tipped into evening, we chatted about the people we knew, the clubs where we had partied. We were drinking mojitos, a mixture of rum, sugar, lime, mint, and cool, crunchy bits of cucumber that I kept fishing out and putting into my mouth. Diamond, who was single, announced she found it difficult to find femmes who would dominate her, and I blurted out, "I'm a top." I knew then I was going to go to bed with her. My heart was racing, and I hadn't experienced that in such a long time. It was like puking when you hadn't done it in years—violent, familiar, and necessary.

The next day at work, I received a delivery of what was

pretty close to a dead porcupine. The quills were going to be used in a class on making moccasins at the museum. I told Beth I was taking the course, and on the day it began, I found myself standing in front of Diamond's apartment building, a concrete low-rise whose ugliness evoked Lego and communism.

The interior door was propped open because the intercom system wasn't working, and I made my way up concrete stairs that smelled like bleach. I was surprised a place like this existed in the fashionable Annex. Diamond told me she always lived in dumpy apartments in perfect neighbourhoods, which was the opposite of what I liked: beautiful, old buildings in run-down neighbourhoods. Diamond herself was that combination of elegance and sketch. She had put on weight (as had I), her now shoulder-length hair had turned silver, and she dressed in thuggish track pants and hoodies, with a navy tuque jammed onto her head. Yet she had retained her severe natural beauty: the luminous skin, the cut-glass cheekbones, and the grey-blue eyes that were a shade I usually only saw on Siberian Huskies.

I had barely sat down when Diamond asked me if I wanted to smoke up. I shook my head while she got out a bong whose base was filled with dark, smudgy water. I hadn't known she was a pothead. Like most addicts, Diamond claimed pot made her normal. In a sense this was true: The pot didn't relax her—she sat at her desk, babbling away about Buddhism. When she paused, I patted the spot next to me on her bed.

"Am I talking too much?" she asked.

I nodded my head. She sat beside me, and we kissed. It felt more pleasant than electric; I was nervous, too.

Then I went into the bathroom and brushed my hair, which I had ironed for the occasion, and put on some dark lipstick and changed into a black lace bra and panties, a garter belt, and stockings. As I fastened my stockings to my garter, I felt myself disassociate, as though I were watching myself star in a porn movie. It had been more than a decade since I had had sex with anyone besides Beth.

When I came out of the bathroom, I saw that Diamond had also stripped down—she was naked except for what appeared to be an enormous pair of hockey kneepads.

I squinted at her—I wasn't wearing my glasses—to make sure I was really seeing a pair of hockey kneepads.

Diamond pranced over to me. "This way I can service you for a long time."

I raised my palms. "Those kneepads have to go."

"But my knees get sore," she protested.

In the end, we found a solution that worked for both of us: her lying on her back with me sitting on her face. Another problem arose: The harness she had was too big for me. Still, I enjoyed myself. The scent of her was intoxicating, her sweat and juices mingled with men's cologne and the acrid tang of pot. Afterwards, as I gathered up my clothes, I told her, "I'd do that again."

"Hell, yeah," she replied. "I'll be your midlife crisis."

I had just turned forty; she was forty-five, like Lisa, like Beth, five years older than me, but she seemed younger.

The day after we slept together, I emailed her, telling her I had fun and wanted to see her again.

She emailed me back: *You fucking me on top was quite yum. I'm having more snaps added to my harness for your lovely slender body cuz next time I want more than your hand. I want you with the big boy, missy.*

I replied: *You want cock? You'll get it, as long as you behave.*

The way we interacted was so raunchy. Diamond had never lived with a lover and couldn't recall how many women she'd slept with. According to her, a lot of them had treated her badly. Not by cheating or lying or abusing or exploiting her. No, their biggest crime was dumping her. Freaking out on her for the pot or for no reason. Yeah, right. She was obviously fucked up. I didn't care. In a way it was a plus. The fact that she was addicted to pot and couldn't sustain relationships meant I would never be tempted to run off with her.

Sex with her felt like a theatrical production, maybe because of her background. As a teenager, she had starred in a Canadian television show that was supposed to be progressive but was actually pretty racist. It was about a boarding school in the Yukon for troubled girls who learned life lessons through encounters with nature and the wisdom of an old Tlingit man. Diamond was the old man's half-white granddaughter (never mind that she didn't have a drop of Aboriginal blood), a tomboy who drove dog sleds. The show had lasted five seasons and was a cult phenomenon in Asia. (Diamond had had a Japanese fan club in the eighties.) Diamond claimed she couldn't act, that she had just played herself, and since then, she'd had a spotty career in the tech side of film and television, creating objects for sets. If a milk carton was needed that didn't have a Canadian company trademark on it, she would make one. Some of her constructions were amazing, but she no longer got much work. Her connections were gone, and the work was now mostly done digitally.

When it came to sex, I was the director while she was in charge of visuals, in particular wardrobe. She liked me to wear pencil skirts and high heels and Bettie-Page style lingerie, so off I went to Kensington Market, and to the Fluevog store where I took out my credit card. (Oddly, I felt guiltier for spending money Beth and I didn't have on shoes than for getting my pussy licked.) I sent Diamond a link to the Fluevog website, where she could admire the vintage-style pumps I had bought for her visual enjoyment.

She texted back immediately: *Wow, those shoes are HOT and HIGH!*

I answered: *Indeed. Think of the threat those heels could pose against soft shoulders if you aren't sufficiently diligent or focused with your mouth. I want to see you hungry, frustrated, vulnerable, and—at the same time—embarrassingly wet.*

Her response came a few hours later: *3 of the 4 requirements have been reached. All are possible.*

I replied: *So what requirement wasn't reached? Let me guess—not vulnerable because you're such a hard-ass.*

She answered: *You got it.* Minutes later: *When can the BOI next serve her LADY?*

I knew I couldn't keep having sex with her, even though it made me more patient with Beth, who told me she was glad I was going out more. I had no idea whether Beth had figured out or cared that I might be having sex—she was still in pretty rough shape—but I knew she would hate how much space Diamond was taking up in my head. When Beth suggested I look elsewhere, I had imagined Craigslist hookups without bothering to read the ads. When I did, I discovered that gay women, if they were over the age of twenty-five, didn't do Craigslist; straight women with boyfriends did, and the pictures they posted of their shaved cunts nestled against ugly couches weren't compelling.

Diamond compelled me though our relationship was odd. Whenever I saw her, she had a fresh crisis. While she never asked for help, her need for it was so obvious I found myself directing her to a legal clinic, getting her a doctor, helping her write a CV. I was her mommy and her whore.

In the bedroom, I became the sort of sophisticated, amoral woman I enjoyed watching in films. I had a trippy moment at the Army Surplus when all I could see was the erotic potential in the items surrounding me: rope to capture Diamond, weapons that could transform me into a scary, sexy Bond girl, the antithesis of a nice lesbian-feminist Quaker. Admittedly, I was only a sporadic attender of Toronto meeting, but being a Quaker was like being a Jew; it was cultural. I was rebelling against my own values of not being selfish, of antimilitarism. Diamond had told me she wanted me to force her, scare her.

"By hurting you? You want me to flog you?" I didn't want to cause pain. I was sick to death of pain.

"No, whipping's too literal," Diamond had said. "I want you to control me like the Dog Whisperer."

I headed for a display case in the Army Surplus store. Texted Diamond that I wanted her to wear a really ugly pair of underwear on our next date.

Okay, she texted.

Curious?

Anxious to live out whatever you're going to do. I'm sure you'll put me to good use.

Two days later, we sat on her bed, fully dressed, kissing. When she reached up to caress my breast, I moved her hand, even though my nipples were hard.

I pointed to the floor. "Lie down!"

Diamond scrambled off the bed and lay on her back on the green carpet. I paced around her in another pair of shoes that dated back to the fifties. (One of the museum curators—gay of course—had taken me to an auction.) My ensemble, inspired by Diamond's fantasies of haughty female executives, included a navy pencil skirt and a burgundy silk blouse. As she studied my outfit, I strutted over and placed one foot on each side of her face.

She gazed up my skirt—she could see my exposed pussy. She gave me a blurry smile and ran her hands along my ankles. "You are seriously smoking."

I glanced pointedly at her hands. "Are you forgetting I'm the boss?"

She released my ankles with a smirk. "Maybe you need to remind me?"

I lifted my heel so it was just above her hand. She was bigger and stronger than me, but in this position I could crush her fingers before she had a chance to move. "I'm in charge." Annoyance crept into my voice. "Wipe that grin off your face."

"Yes, ma'am," she murmured, still smiling.

I gave her hair a sharp tug and held it tightly in my fist. Watched the smugness drain from her face. "Are you going to do what I say?"

"Yes." Diamond stared at me as if she didn't know what had hit her. Then, in a whisper, "I'm so wet."

The toe of my shoe prodded the area between her legs. "Are you sure you know your place?"

She bit her lip. "Beneath you."

I pressed my shoe into her, and she moaned. I continued to toy with her, making her pant.

She asked, "Want me to do something for you?"

"You are," I replied, deliberately misunderstanding. What she wanted was to lick me. I wanted to make her wait. I ordered her to get undressed and lie on her stomach.

She wriggled out of her T-shirt and jeans. No bra and the requisite ugly undergarments: tight purple briefs. The wetness between her legs had visibly soaked through the fabric, and the sight of her arousal made me want to put my fingers inside her.

When she was sprawled across the bed, I put my hand between her legs and felt her dampness. Her body tensed as she made a visible effort to keep herself from grinding against me.

"Close your eyes," I told her.

She did, and I took a knife out of my purse. Pushed up my skirt and sat on her back, pressing the wet heat of my pussy into the area where her buttocks fanned out. I unsheathed the knife. It was small and sharp with a pearl handle. From working as a cook, I knew dull knives were more dangerous than sharp ones. I told her to open her eyes.

Diamond turned her head. Her eyes widened, and surprise rippled across her face. The female executive had turned into an assassin. She didn't seem afraid. The funny thing was I felt afraid. I hadn't realized how much I enjoyed sexual power. How far would her submission take me?

Diamond mouthed, "Be careful."

"I'm not going to hurt you."

I gestured for her to turn over, and laid the blade against one side of her underwear and cut it off. I had thought I might have to hack away at it, but in two smooth motions I cut off the briefs. After putting the knife away, I picked up the scraps and loosely gagged her with them. She moaned with pleasure, and confidence surged through me. I jammed my fingers into her hot, slippery cunt. When she began to buck, I removed my hand. Took the underwear out of Diamond's mouth.

"You liked being violated, didn't you?"

"Oh God, you don't know how much. Well..." Diamond paused. "You kind of do." She rolled over on her back and grinned at me. "Did you like it?"

"Can't you tell?" I began to undress. When I was down to a half-girdle and stockings, I straddled Diamond's face. Thrust my cunt against her mouth, her chin.

"Get me off," I told her.

She licked me with an awkward hunger, her mouth wide open, her tongue stretched out as far as it could go.

My orgasm felt like a gong, vibrations of pleasure repeatedly striking the walls of my cunt.

When I finally stopped coming, Diamond looked up at me from between my legs. Her face was red and sweaty. "That was mind-blowing."

"It was." I felt dazed. "But it's not over yet. I still want to fuck you."

"Trust me, I want you to. But we can take a break." Diamond padded out of bed to retrieve her bong and lighter. She took a few hits and held the bong out to me. For the first time, I nodded.

"Open your mouth," she said.

I opened it, and she took a hit and sealed her mouth over mine to blow the smoke inside. I held it in my lungs for a moment and exhaled. We did this a few times.

"Diamond, were you okay with the knife?"

"It made me a little nervous," she admitted. "I was worried you might hurt me accidentally."

I giggled. "You're the first person I've pulled a knife on during sex."

"Really? You seemed like you knew what you were doing. It's strange, but when you dominate me, I feel safe."

When she said this, she sounded wistful. I leaned over and stroked her forehead. She was covered in sweat, which embarrassed her but didn't bother me. Her vulnerability made me feel protective. Also, like her, I found psychological satisfaction in our games. Domination calmed the tide of my thoughts and left me feeling peaceful.

I was ready for another round. I got on top of her, and we started kissing. I lightly touched her sensitive nipples, and she started to breathe hard.

"Please fuck me," she said.

I peeled off my stockings and put on Diamond's dildo and harness. Her black leather harness had a lot of complicated straps, and I felt like a horse being saddled up. At home, I had a more elegant, feminine harness that was like a G-string, but I preferred not to wear with Diamond what I wore with Beth.

While I tightened the buckles, Diamond lifted her legs into the air. Her gestures were utterly masculine, but when I fucked her, she would flip her legs way up, like a Barbie doll. I loved the way she was one thing hidden inside another.

"You had better fuck me so good that I feel it until the next time I see you," Diamond said.

I kissed her knee for an answer. It was the first time she had said anything that suggested she missed me, and it made me happy to know she felt the same way about me as I did about her. I gripped her ankles and put them against my shoulders and slid my cock into her and screwed her. I felt like a teenage boy, which was fun, but I shifted into coy girl mode.

"You like my cock, don't you, baby?" I teased.

"Yes, yes." She rubbed her nipples, which meant she wanted me to touch them.

I bent over and licked them and began to fuck her more slowly.

"Don't stop, don't stop." Diamond began to finger herself, and I felt her legs shudder. This was my cue to slam the dick deep inside her, and I did and she came, stuffing her pillow against her mouth to muffle her cries.

When she had finished, I noticed the red numbers on the clock radio above her bed. Diamond, catching my gaze, shook her head. "It's late, eh? Sexing it up with you is such a time warp."

"Yeah," I agreed. I had once banged drugs with my old buddy Donny. I never forgot the experience, puking up sour juice followed by a rush flowing through me like smoke billowing from a stack.

I nodded out, and before I knew it, the high was over. Hours had passed, and I thought, *Too soon, and, I want more.* This was what Diamond made me feel—joy followed by the yearning for more, more, more.

I unbuckled the harness and left the room to take a shower. When I got out of the bathroom, Diamond handed me my clothes.

As I fastened my bra, she asked, "Are you going to be upset if I don't fall for you?"

I laughed.

She looked a little pissed off. "What's so funny?"

I didn't answer. I felt she was being arrogant about what she assumed I wanted and naïve in thinking that people can decide what they will or won't feel.

Diamond picked up her cell, her tone coldly business-like when she asked, "Should I call you a cab?"

"Please."

I kissed her and headed to the lobby. I had gone down one flight of stairs when I noticed I'd forgotten my purse. I ran back up to her apartment and knocked on the door.

When she opened the door, she was holding my purse. She silently watched me take it, and I thought, *She's lonely.* In an acute way, I felt her loneliness, like a meaty internal organ, deep, hidden, fundamental.

Usually, I sent a post-coital email to Diamond, but when I woke up the next morning, I saw she'd beat me to it. It was the longest email I had received from her. It began: *You topped me divinely. I gave you more power than I have ever given anyone, and it was the best kind of narcotic.* It continued in this vein for several paragraphs before concluding: *I care for you.*

I replied: *You care for me. How cautious of you. Sex with you was indeed delicious, some of the best of my life.*

She answered: *Same for me. I can't wait to see you, touch you, taste you again, woman.*

This was getting hard. I accepted the risk of her, intuitively knew that it was a danger that could be survived. For me, everything came down to time: When would we see each other again? When would I have to give her up? Our relationship existed in the present tense, which was where she lived. She didn't have any real responsibilities. She had come back to Toronto because her mother was dying, and within a month of Diamond's return, her mother had died.

A day later, I got another email from her. This one was a fragmented description of a party: *Huge gay boy house party, big condo downtown, dj, lots of coke. Some women showed up. One chick hit on me forcefully.*

Diamond often reported incidents of people hitting on her. People were attracted to her partly because of her appearance and partly because she lacked boundaries—she would discuss sex in detail with almost anybody. She had recently been surprised when she was hanging out with a guy whom she had met at her dealer's house and the guy thought they were on a date. "I'm gay," she had told him in astonishment. "You need to think of me as a dude."

But the next time I saw Diamond, the first thing she blurted out was, "I feel like I cheated on you." She had brought home the woman who was coming on to her at the party. The woman had been too drunk to drive home and asked to crash at her place, and Diamond let her but swore all they had done was make out.

I ran my hands through my hair while thinking, *Fuck.* We hadn't discussed Diamond dating other women. It would be hypocritical of me to expect her not to date. Still, it stung.

I sighed. "You could have talked to me first."

Diamond's mouth tightened. "Call you at home while you're with your wife to ask if I could fuck someone?"

I sat down on Diamond's chair and didn't answer. I didn't want to think about how we would break up.

Now she whined, "I just took off her shirt and licked her nipples. I told her I was too drunk to fuck. Don't you believe me?"

Did I? I believed she'd rather have sex with me.

Diamond hugged herself. "I couldn't because I kept thinking about you. I can't stop thinking about you."

She sounded so surprised and miserable that I suddenly did believe her. I got up and put my arms around her; she was shaking. "That's worse in a way," I said. "I'm hurting you. You should dump me."

But she didn't, and I didn't. Her next few emails were less porno and mine were less arch. Hers were signed "Hungry Loverboi" and "Big Bear Hugs and Kisses," while mine were simply signed "love."

I needed to talk to someone, so I arranged a drink with Veronika, who once told me I was her favourite person to discuss sex with. These days, I heard about her travel adventures. Every few months, she and Jiang popped off somewhere: Jamaica, Budapest, Ibiza, Bali, Buenos Aires. Jiang was loaded. They had new friends, gay men who could keep up with their lifestyle. Some of them worked, as Veronika now did, coordinating big charity events. I also had new friends. Beth's best friend had moved back to Toronto, and we hung out with her and her girlfriend: They were nerdy and as obsessed with *Buffy the Vampire Slayer* as we were.

Sitting in Motel, a half-hipster, half-dive bar where the lamps were askew and the piano was being played badly, I was grateful for Veronika's company. She didn't judge, and I was glad of it.

"I guess you needed to go there." She grinned at me. "I didn't know Diamond was all submissive and shit. And I guess that's why we fizzled—we're both bottoms."

"The lexicon has shifted. Top and bottom now refer to who does what to whom physically," I said. "Submissive and dominant describe your state of mind."

"You're such a librarian." Veronika poked at her lime with a straw. "So is Diamond payback for Lisa?"

"For fuck's sake," I said. "No!" Maybe I was reliving my youth a bit, getting to be Veronika this time, the girl who bagged the hottest ones, the girl who didn't care about consequences.

The day after our drink, the hospital called to say Beth should come for surgery. This wasn't scheduled for another six weeks, but we had spent enough time in the health care system to know opportunities had to be seized. After waiting at the hospital for several hours, my wife was ushered into a corridor lined with hospital beds. Shower curtains encircled the beds, allowing for a modicum of privacy. I sat on the bed while Beth took off her clothes.

"Damn," she said.

"What?"

She sighed. "I'm wearing boxer shorts. The last time I was here, the nurses looked at me like I was a freak when they saw my underwear."

My heart crunched. For almost two years, pain had devoured Beth's body. I had almost become inured to the sound of her moaning, was capable of fetching her morphine tablets in my sleep, but this new humiliation scraped at me.

I stroked my wife's slender arm sticking out of the blue hospital gown. She was right beside me, and I missed her so damn much. What the fuck was I doing with Diamond? "If you want, I can go get you some plain cotton women's underwear."

"No, that's okay."

I refused to have sex with Diamond while Beth was in the hospital. Instead, we grabbed lunch at Diamond's favourite Indian buffet, where she wouldn't let me hold her hand. I didn't realize she was serious until she shoved her hands under the table.

"You've got to be kidding."

She said, "The people here wouldn't like that sort of thing."

The prim disapproval was genuine. I realized Diamond was one of those dykes who wished she wasn't one. Being cautious if you were risking a beating was one thing; caring more about making homophobes comfortable than your partner's feelings was quite another. Except Diamond wasn't my partner—she was my mistress.

I wasn't sure what I was to her. Today I was going to a storage space with her to sort through her mother's boxes. A mother who used to call her every week to tell her to change her life, get a boyfriend. I tried to help Diamond decide what to throw away, what to keep, what to give to the Salvation Army, but she was too distracted. Rambled on about a lamp her mom had bought, the nice doorman at the apartment they had when she was on the TV show.

"Maybe we should do this another time," I suggested.

"Do you have to go see Beth? I know she needs you, too."

"I'm seeing her tonight. What I meant was you don't seem to want to do this right now."

Diamond sighed. "It's so hard for me. You can't imagine. I have a lot of anger about my situation."

I stared at Diamond, who didn't sound angry. The way she sometimes talked about her feelings was weird, as if they were shapes she was identifying on a chart.

"It sucks having no family, no support system to help me through this."

She had a family; she just didn't get along with them. Diamond's mother had been her father's mistress, and neither her father nor her half-siblings wanted much to do with her. Still, Diamond knew lots of people. The city was littered with her ex-girlfriends.

I teased her. "Poor you. You have to depend upon the kindness of strangers."

"I do, I do," she insisted with an unexpected grin.

On top of a frothy pile of polyester nightgowns was a

framed picture of an older woman, and I picked it up. The woman had dyed black hair, pink lipstick, and the same pale eyes as Diamond, but the expression in them was different—assessing rather than waiting to be assessed.

Diamond stuck her hand out, and I gave her the picture. She looked at it longingly. "Mummy always took care of herself, went to an aesthetician every week. It was good she was so out of it at the nursing home. She would have been horrified by how they didn't bathe her and left her in diapers." She blinked and set the picture on the floor.

This was the first time I had seen Diamond grieve the death of her mother. I put my hand on her shoulder.

"I didn't realize how bad she'd got. One of her friends called me, and I came out here. Her mouth was full of blood. Her teeth and gums were all red and brown and yellow, but they didn't give a shit at that home. No one did anything about it, I'm telling you, no one, no one, no one."

Diamond's voice had risen, was almost tearful. She was sad and pissed off and ashamed. Ashamed *she* hadn't taken better care of her mother. She couldn't admit that to me, probably not even to herself. Her shame was like shiny wet blots of ink on a dark screen, hard to make out but smeared over everything in her life.

I watched her with a worried expression, and she squeezed me. "You're a doll for helping me."

At that moment, it was she who reminded me of a doll, one of those ones where you pull a string and hear them laugh, then cry, then do something else. As if her feelings were too overwhelming for her to stay with them for any length of time.

When Beth got home from the hospital, she told me she couldn't wait to have sex with me, that she'd missed it terribly. Even after the pain began, Beth liked to do me now and then for the closeness.

I burst into tears. When I couldn't stop, she said, "You're sleeping with someone." She said, "I don't fucking believe this."

"You said I could have casual sex and to not tell you," I sobbed.

"But it's not casual, is it?"

I couldn't answer, and Beth glared at me. "Shit."

She see-sawed between blaming me and blaming herself. I told her it wasn't that complicated; part of the affair had to do with her illness, and part of it had nothing to do with her.

I offered to break it off, but Beth surprised me by saying no. "One, you'll resent me. Two, this is normal for you; your parents have an open marriage."

With a permission I didn't examine too closely, I resumed having sex with Diamond while reading books about how to have an open relationship. It seemed as if I'd broken the rules, that affairs couldn't be turned into poly. The triangle I was in was an isosceles, with the lines of desire decidedly unequal.

I called my parents and asked them about their marriage. My mother had had a ten-year relationship with an anthropology professor, Nils, a large man with a fuzzy grey beard who always seemed to be dressed in brown wide-wale corduroys with sandals and wool socks. He was also married with kids. I'd met his family once when I was thirteen or fourteen, on a clam digging expedition. The clams hadn't been the regular white ones. They were razor clams, which were black and shiny and pinched your fingers when they shot deeper into the wet sand, out of the reach of a grasping hand. Part of me had wanted to capture the clams, part of me wanted to leave them alone, which was how I'd felt about my parents' marriage, curious and also as if I didn't want to know. My father didn't seem to have girlfriends. Was he a loser being taken advantage of by my mother?

Now I asked questions. My mother was somewhat embarrassed ("It was the times"), whereas my father, who had had only one outside relationship, was proud ("It was what we believed in, what our heroes, the Bloomsbury Group, believed in"). Nils' relationship with my mother collapsed when he got involved with a doctoral student. That relationship had been short-lived, and eventually Nils and my mother resumed a friendship.

Beth and I started fucking again, and it was great. But when we weren't having sex, we were fighting. We started seeing a counsellor. I said what I'd missed with Beth while she was ill wasn't sex so much as joy, and Diamond had given me that. Witnessing Beth's pain had been hard.

"Not as hard as going through it," Beth retorted.

I persisted. "Whenever our dogs have the slightest upset, you insist on whisking them off to the vet. You hate seeing them suffer."

"Okay, I get what you're saying," Beth said.

Later that day, our understanding evaporated. We fought over my forgetting to pick up Diet Coke for her, and she called me a cheating, betraying slut. I slapped her. It was shocking to both of us. How had we become these figures from a Jerry Springer show?

I called Holly, who told me I should know she was no relationship expert. She and Dana had this "it's complicated" relationship. They had split up and got back together. They continued to live separately—Dana's fastidiousness and desire for alone time didn't work with Holly's extended family and sociability.

"This is a social-worker-who-has-done-a-lot-of-assessments question," I told Holly. "Who is the real Beth? The reasonable person in the therapist's office who says, 'I like knowing my marriage is strong enough to handle affairs', or the person who picks fights with me every day and just called me a slut?"

Holly said, "The person who called you a slut."

"Fuck." That meant I had to break up with Diamond. I was making Beth crazy and couldn't give Diamond what she wanted: If I loved them, I had no choice but to make a choice.

First I told Beth, who was relieved. She said, "I didn't know I could be that jealous."

I called Diamond the next day. She spat out words as ugly as Beth's had been earlier: "Was that just your pussy talking when you told me you loved me?"

I felt a momentary impulse to laugh at what seemed like a ridiculous miscast of me as the thuggish boy and her as the innocent girl who had been taken for a ride.

"You know it wasn't like that," I replied. *Was it?*

"I'm in love with you," Diamond insisted in a dramatic tone.

I didn't believe her. She needed me more than she loved me, while Beth was the opposite. Beth had crawled into her physical pain like it was a shell and refused to ask for help or admit defeat. What she and Diamond had in common was their pride and the idea that it was wrong to have needs.

A few days later, I cycled over to Diamond's apartment. As she lay on her bed, taking puffs from her bong, I told her, "You really have to quit smoking dope if you want a quality woman. Otherwise, you'll get addicts or women who want to rescue you." It wasn't the time to nag, but I was feeling defensive.

She blew smoke out. "Is that what you are? Someone who wants to rescue me?"

"Please, I'm no martyr. You of all people should know that." I sat on the end of her bed. "But I care about you. I'd like to see you get your shit together."

Diamond looked at me like she understood something. "That's why you got involved with me, isn't it?" She held up her bong. "Because I'm a drug addict. You were protecting your relationship."

I nodded. "Wasn't that obvious?"

"No," she said in a small voice.

I stretched out my legs so they rested against hers. "I thought that was at least as obvious as the appeal of my unavailability."

She didn't reply. When I hugged her, she hugged me back tightly. I started to cry. I was going to miss her; I was going to miss this.

We had sex then. Started to, anyway. I kissed her, and she pulled away her mouth. "I don't want you to kiss me."

I felt like a straight guy sleeping with a prostitute who had said kissing wasn't allowed. She was mad at me, contemptuous.

She grabbed my hand. "You can still fuck me."

"No," I said. "No, I can't."

Safe Space

Toronto, 2014

I met Beth in the lobby of the Gladstone, a boutique hotel at the edge of Parkdale. Once a flophouse, the Gladstone had been reinvented as an artistic and cultural space. A porter led us to the elevator, a Victorian brass cage with mirrors in it. From there we were taken to an artist-designed room with a film-noir ambiance. Bars of pink neon lights bathed the room in a glow, softening the dark wallpaper and brass lamps heavy enough to be used as murder weapons. The décor was a naughty fantasy and strangely appropriate for our weekend plans—Beth and I were attending Sanctuary, a queer women and trans kink event.

While Beth showered, I opened the doors of the enormous black lacquer wardrobe and hung up a confection of silk and velvet. Unbuckled my pumps, kicked them into a corner, and stripped off my blouse and skirt. Ripped free the bedspread to run my hands along the white cotton sheets. I had a fetish for hotel rooms, probably a result of the passionate encounters I'd had in them with Lisa all those years ago.

I was lying in bed when Beth stepped out in a towel. As she came towards me, I tugged at the towel. She removed my hand.

"Do you think our dogs will be okay? Do you think Sophia will be able to handle them for the entire weekend?"

I sighed. Veronika described Beth as having an attachment parenting style when it came to our dogs. "I'm sure our dogs are perfectly safe. And if, by chance, something goes wrong, we're mere blocks and a text away." I stood up to take my shower—the opening ceremony was in less than an hour.

Sanctuary was being held in the basement of a community centre a block from the Gladstone, where most of the participants were staying. Unlike our hotel, the community centre was anything but hip. It looked like, well, a community centre in a lower income neighbourhood—frayed carpet, table by the door with name tags and two women collecting money and tickets, folding chairs in front of a riser, and lots of mismatched furniture.

The evening began with speeches. People and sponsors were thanked, and rules were spelled out. No drugs or alcohol were allowed on the premises, and dungeon monitors would intervene if they thought there was a problem. Sanctuary was a safe space that included a no-play area where people could emotionally recharge and a separate room with stronger lighting and first aid kits for blood play.

Blood play? The idea made me want to curl up into a fetal position. Had it been a mistake to come here? The masters of ceremonies referred to the crowd as fellow perverts, and that was fine, except I didn't feel like one. The pleasure I took in telling my partners what to do seemed banal; being a lesbian was more anomalous. Was this the right place for me, for Beth?

We had come to explore. Were there activities we'd never done but might enjoy? Ways to be non-monogamous that weren't as complicated as poly or as painful as an affair? My relationship with Diamond had hurt all of us, yet neither Beth nor I thought the answer was necessarily monogamy.

Regular sex with Beth wasn't always going to be possible. Beth's arthritis had turned out to be a nameless immune disorder. The ear infections and sore throats she sometimes got were related. The deterioration she had experienced in her knees was travelling to other parts of her body. There was no cure, just the management of pain—if fighting the misery and helplessness of pain could be called managing.

The speeches were followed by an auction. At the door, Beth and I had been provided with chocolate coins to bid on services—whippings, canings, bootblacking. A young femme decked out in an old-fashioned virginal white gown got up on stage and offered up a lap dance. Her damsel-in-distress look intrigued me. Almost every other femme in the place was either wearing a black dress or lingerie, and I appreciated the original style of the damsel in distress and the way her outfit hinted at her desire, which I read as submissive. Looking at her took me back to when I was first coming out and sleeping with femme bottoms. Not that I'd understood that then.

An intense bidding war erupted for fisting services from a large black woman wearing a cop uniform. I had once bought a cop's shirt and pants in Kensington Market and worn them with Diamond, who was up for a fantasy of resisting arrest and being subdued. I'd felt as if I was in a bad Halloween costume. Every line out of my mouth was a ridiculous cliché, and our scene had degenerated into hilarity.

Diamond had begun dating shortly after our split, and I got mad at her for telling me in detail about her sex life with her new girlfriend. "You're jealous," she said triumphantly. She thought I still wanted her. I didn't because she didn't want me. She was no longer holding up a mirror that told me something I had never objectively believed: that I was beautiful. What I wanted was to travel back in time to what we'd had.

Beth nudged me into the present. The auction had ended, and women were stacking up the rows of chairs. As I put my own chair away, a trans woman, naked except for a giant red cape, squished past me. She hadn't had bottom surgery.

I caught Beth's eye. "Am I an asshole for not wanting to see a penis?"

Beth shrugged. "Well, it is a queer women and *trans* space."

Was it that big a deal? Was it more or less of a turn off than cisgender women I found unattractive or who acted like assholes? When it came down to it, there were few women I wanted to have sex with or even watch have sex, facts that were at odds with the ideal of an inclusive space.

Back in our film noir hotel room at the Gladstone, Beth and I analyzed our reactions to the evening. We'd had to coax women around us into social niceties. I'd thought

Sanctuary might be an opportunity for Beth to fool around with someone, but we'd be lucky to even make friends. Something about the evening worked for us though because we had urgent sex in a blur of pink neon light.

The next morning, we headed down Queen Street and were accosted by young women soliciting donations for the Because I am a Girl charity.

"You two look like friendly people," one of them fake-complimented us.

"Actually, we're incredibly hostile," I replied dryly. I was sympathetic to their cause but not their approach. I hadn't even had coffee yet.

They burst into laughter, which made me grin sheepishly. Beth and I ducked into a bistro. Over French toast with brandy-soaked apricots and faultless cappuccinos, we examined the workshop schedule. Branding? Ouch. 24-7 master/slave relationships? Nope. What about something called Sacred and Cathartic Power Exchange?

"My aspirations aren't that high," I said. "I like sex that's fun. Ideally, naughty fun."

"There's a bondage workshop. Or we could have sex." Beth reached under the small table and skimmed a hand under my blouse.

We did both. At the bondage workshop, we were the only couple in which the femme tied up the masculine person. We whispered to each other about it. Was dominant butch or dominant trans guy / submissive femme the reality, or were masculine people too embarrassed to be seen being tied up? As "novices," we didn't know. With helpful instruction from Beth, I mastered the knots before anyone else did. Beth jerked her hands but was unable to get out of her bonds. "This is cool."

"I'm too lazy to do it all the time," I said. Handcuffs were easier.

The people around me didn't share my feelings. They held forth on the quality and craftsmanship of hemp and how to choose the right carabiner while my mind drifted.

Nonetheless, when we returned to our room, we experimented with the terrycloth ties on the hotel-supplied bathrobes and wound up having sex for the third time that day. I couldn't understand our horniness since we were approaching the weekend activities with such critical detachment.

Veggie hotdogs from a street vendor took the edge off our more prosaic hunger. Then it was time to shower and dress for the main event, a play party. Beth put on a fresh black T-shirt and jeans while I wore a low-cut black top and bottle-green velvet skirt. We had considered buying fetish clothes, but since we didn't wear them generally, it seemed silly and as if we were trying too hard. Maybe we should have. At the party, nearly everyone was in black leather.

I looked around for the damsel in distress, wondering what she was wearing. Practically nothing it turned out, since she was getting fucked. She and another femme were squished into an armchair, both facing forward, with the damsel in distress sliding up and down on a dildo strapped to the other woman's thigh. They were attentive to each other while enjoying the thrill of being watched.

"I find them hotter than anything else going on," I whispered to Beth.

"Unlike most of the people here, they look like they're

having fun," she murmured. Around us people were whipping each other in a solemn, methodical manner that reminded me of metronomes. It was like watching people chop wood.

I went to the washroom. On my way back, I stopped to observe a threesome. An energetic trans woman bound her cisgender lover to a chair, stuck a gag in her mouth, and began fist-fucking a third woman. The couple was blonde with porn-star looks while their hookup was a curvy brunette.

Someone tapped my shoulder. It was the dungeon monitor, who told me I was standing too close to the women. I didn't think I was but took a step back, and the dungeon monitor continued her patrol of the play area.

A little later, the curvy brunette wandered by, and I told her, "You seemed like you were having a good time."

She blushed charmingly. "You noticed!" (Clearly, she hadn't been too oppressed by my gaze.) She rooted around in a black handbag and brought out a joint. "You guys want to go outside and smoke this with me?"

"Sure," I said.

We were grateful to have somebody talk to us. We headed out to the parking lot, where a few other women were smoking ordinary cigarettes. We blazed up with the brunette, who flirted with Beth. I didn't mind. In fact, I felt flattered.

On our way back inside, Beth murmured to me, "She's obviously into couples. You know we could fuck her."

"I'll pass. Go for it if you want to," I said. Strange girls had once been an incredible adventure. Now they felt like a chore.

"It's enough to know I can, that someone is interested in me," Beth said. "It's annoying you aren't more jealous."

"Sorry," I said. "Seriously, go ahead."

"Unfortunately, I just want to have sex with you."

Inside, we chatted with a couple from the bondage workshop. Assorted activities crossed my field of vision: covered and bare asses being flogged and caned; a redhead with large breasts and an apron around her middle serving cupcakes; two fat naked butches with Mexican wrestling masks locked in combat on blue gym mats.

A butch and a femme who were our age, with a much younger boi in tow, came over to where we were standing and moved furniture out of the way. When they had cleared some space, the femme directed the boi to take off her pants. The boi dropped to the floor and obeyed. She looked even younger in her T-shirt and briefs, and she had a purple bruise the size of a dinner plate on her thigh. As soon as she stood up, the grey-haired butch, who had put on a pair of red boxing gloves, punched her. Repeatedly. The boi howled with pain. It was real violence, fast, brutal, and shimmery, nothing like the flogging, no gradual pushing of the body's limits. The femme alternated between yelling abuse at the boi and hugging her.

Beth said, "I know this is consensual, but I'm creeped out by Mean Mommy and the Family Abuse Scene."

"Me, too."

The women around us also looked uncomfortable. One of them gestured towards the boi and said, "The submissive is being punched in her sternum. That's not safe."

I stopped averting my eyes long enough to realize this was true. The femme smirked. She was enjoying our discomfort. Her scene seemed less about desire and more about proving she was the most hardcore player in the room. I wasn't at a knitting convention, but what I was willing to tolerate was not the same as what I accepted—a distinction every queer understood.

I asked Beth if she wanted to stay.

"I was going to ask you the same question."

Back at the hotel, we raided the mini-bar. Poured teeny bottles of spirits into plastic cups and got into bed with our drinks. Beth popped a painkiller.

"You know what I don't understand about tonight?"

Beth hit her palm against her forehead. "Just one thing?"

"Ha, ha," I said. "What I want to know is why did the dungeon monitor reprimand me for standing too close to the women having sex and not say a word to the butch with the boxing gloves?"

"You're easy to take on. You're not part of the scene."

It was possible the dungeon monitor knew more about those women than we did, or maybe Beth was right and she was a hypocrite. I expected more of queers, which was dumb. It wasn't as though we were superior—or inferior for that matter—we just were. We're here, we're queer, get used to it was what I'd grown up with, was different from the current demands for safe space. Demands I wasn't entirely comfortable with because who defined safe and when did it rub up against freedom?

I understood wanting a safe space—any person who has been treated like shit would. Safety was the price I'd demanded from Beth to be her wife. And when she stroked the centre of my back, as she was right now, I felt utterly safe, precious, protected. When something crappy happened, I wanted Beth the way a two-year-old wants their mom, something I'd never felt about anyone else, something I could barely stand to admit. But being safe, like being happy (and I was very happy at this moment), was temporal. What was more important was being able to handle what comes—whether it was safe or unsafe, weird or ordinary.

CPSIA information can be obtained
at www.ICGtesting.com
Printed in the USA
LVOW13s0542150817
545028LV00001BA/1/P